...ut a more
resourceful woman.

He leaned against the door frame, let the light that stretched into the hall from the living room fall softly across her face and watched the steady rise and fall of her chest. She'd kept a vehicle hidden in a remote location for a quick getaway in the event she was caught. He wondered how many petrol stations and how many routes she had scouted out to ensure she could escape from a variety of locations. She appeared to know every tree and trail in those woods off the interstate. He wouldn't even hazard to guess how many other escape routes she had around the town she'd called home for the past year.

She was absolutely amazing.

She'd gone to great lengths to protect herself and her child. That alone made him wonder about the threat her ex posed…

The Hidden Heir
DEBRA WEBB

INTRIGUE

All the characters in this book have no existence outside the
imagination of the author, and have no relation whatsoever to anyone
bearing the same name or names. They are not even distantly inspired
by any individual known or unknown to the author, and all the
incidents are pure invention.

All Rights Reserved including the right of reproduction in whole or
in part in any form. This edition is published by arrangement with
Harlequin Enterprises II B.V./S.à.r.l. The text of this publication or
any part thereof may not be reproduced or transmitted in any form
or by any means, electronic or mechanical, including photocopying,
recording, storage in an information retrieval system, or otherwise,
without the written permission of the publisher.

This book is sold subject to the condition that it shall not, by way of
trade or otherwise, be lent, resold, hired out or otherwise circulated
without the prior consent of the publisher in any form of binding or
cover other than that in which it is published and without a similar
condition including this condition being imposed on the subsequent
purchaser.

First published in Great Britain 2007
Harlequin Mills & Boon Limited,
Eton House, 18-24 Paradise Road, Richmond, Surrey TW9 1SR

© Debra Webb 2006

ISBN: 978 0 263 85723 8

46-0607

Printed and bound in Spain
by Litografia Rosés S.A., Barcelona

As a mother I have often worried what would become of my youngest daughter if something were to happen to me and her father. I am certain I could count on my eldest daughter as well as my niece, but beyond family, who could I depend on for this enormous obligation? In this life there are friends and there are *friends*. Donna Boyd is a *friend* with whom I would without hesitation trust my daughter's life. This book is dedicated to her unending loyalty and immense kindness. I will forever hold her friendship dear to my heart.

DEBRA WEBB

was born in Scottsboro, Alabama, to parents who taught her that anything is possible if you want it badly enough. She began writing at age nine. Eventually she met and married the man of her dreams, and tried some other occupations, including selling vacuum cleaners, working in a factory, a day-care centre, a hospital and a department store. When her husband joined the military, they moved to Berlin, Germany, and Debra became a secretary in the commanding general's office. By 1985 they were back in the States, and finally moved to Tennessee, to a small town where everyone knows everyone else. With the support of her husband and two beautiful daughters, Debra took up writing again, looking to mystery and films for inspiration. In 1998, her dream of writing for Mills & Boon came true. You can write to Debra with your comments at PO Box 64, Huntland, Tennessee 37345, USA or visit her website at www.debrawebb.com to find out exciting news about her next book.

CAST OF CHARACTERS

Keith Devers – This is his first field assignment. Can a guy who has worked in research his entire career cut it in the field?

Ashley Orrick – Seemingly sweet and vulnerable, she's willing to go to great lengths to keep her son away from his father. But is the money her only motivation?

Desmond Van Valkenberg – His fortune can buy him anything except a cure for his terminal illness. Doesn't he have the right to know his only son?

Mr Brody – Van Valkenberg's personal lawyer. His loyalty lies with his client. How far is he willing to go to keep that client happy?

Ben Haygood – The Top Gun of software and hardware at the Colby Agency. Will he be able to come through for Keith when a life hangs in the balance?

Mary Orrick – Is she protecting her daughter or seeking revenge against the man she hates?

Chapter One

Victoria Colby-Camp sat in the coffee shop on the first floor of the building she called her second home. The place where the Colby Agency had been born, where it thrived more than twenty years later.

Located mere blocks off Chicago's glorious Magnificent Mile, coming to work every day was a treat for the senses. She loved the excitement of the city. Her city. The sounds and smells; the good and the bad that went along with living in an ever-expanding metropolis.

She should be getting back to the office. Lucas—she smiled—would be wondering where she'd gotten to. Every woman who had loved and lost, whatever the circumstances, should have a second chance at the kind of love she had found with Lucas Camp.

Victoria thanked God every day for him, as well as for the health and well-being of her family.

She sipped her Earl Grey and studied the patrons

swarming in and out of the small coffee shop. There were only six tables, each with two delicately formed wrought iron chairs. The seats weren't cushioned, most likely to prevent anyone from growing too comfortable. The owner needn't have worried; most who entered the shop were in a hurry. They were either in a rush to get to work or simply needed to get away from the office for a few moments. Smoking was no longer permitted in the building, so those who partook were forced to go outside to do so.

Of course, there was coffee and tea of all sorts in the lounge on the fourth floor just down the hall from Victoria's office. Or Mildred, her secretary, would have been happy to see after her refreshment needs. Each morning when Victoria came to work, she found coffee, her favorite blend, waiting for her in an elegant carafe. Mildred had a kind of sixth sense when it came to anticipating the needs of most everyone at the agency. This one had been no different.

But, like those with cigarettes and lighters in hand, this morning Victoria had come down to the lobby for a different reason. Escape, for only a minute or two. She couldn't say precisely why she had felt the need. All was well at home and in the office. She simply needed a few moments, not necessarily alone but to herself.

She watched the men and women rush through the main entrance and across the expanse of polished marble floor only to have to wait in line while security scrutinized their possessions as well as their persons. To move beyond that checkpoint, one had to have proper identification and be thoroughly screened for anything that might be used as a weapon.

It was a nuisance, but unfortunately a necessary one in today's climate of unrest.

Victoria settled her attention back on the swiftly cooling tea. Maybe the reason for her desire to have a moment alone was more apparent than she realized. For the first time in almost two decades, everything in her life was exactly as it should be. Her son Jim and his wife Tasha, were at long last happy, and the first Colby grandchild was on the way. The horrors that had haunted Jim since his return home were now finally under control.

A smile toyed with the corners of Victoria's mouth. And her other baby, her agency, was better than ever. She'd hired more new recruits, bringing the total to five. The energy from those young men and women had provided just the transfusion of excitement the agency had needed recently.

Unstoppable.

That was the one word that truly defined her agency as it moved toward its third decade of operation.

She felt completely satisfied for the first time in far too long a time. Satisfied and extremely lucky.

That smile that had tickled her lips now spread

across her face as she caught sight of her husband in the lobby. Confidence radiating from him, Lucas strode straight into the coffee shop. He didn't glance her way, but she knew he was aware of her presence. When his turn in line came, he placed his order— coffee, the strongest Colombian blend, no doubt. Cup in hand, he bypassed the side counter holding various sweeteners and creamers and headed directly for her table. That determined gaze settled on hers and that special connection that bound them so inextricably hummed at its full intensity.

"Is this seat taken?"

She looked up at the man she loved more than life itself and let her smile speak for her. Her husband's own lips quirked as he lowered himself into the seat. The tailored pin-striped suit he wore was her favorite. The blue shirt and deeper navy tie turned his silvery eyes to a warmer hue of passionate gray, making her feel warm and safe inside.

Lucas surveyed the dwindling comings and goings, then rested his full attention on her. "It's kind of early for a break, isn't it?"

That much was true. It wasn't even nine yet. This man had spent the past twenty plus years worrying about her. Even now, when life was as good as it gets, he didn't relent.

"It's been a long time, Lucas, since I've sat and watched life happen around me. I've been so busy trying to keep my world from shattering at every turn that I couldn't risk taking note of anything else." It felt good to be able to step back and just enjoy life as it happened.

He nodded knowingly. "You're afraid it won't last."

Victoria frowned, performing a quick inventory of her feelings. "To some degree, I suppose that's a fair assessment." She picked up her tea, held it with both hands and relished its warmth. However strong she might be, no one was exempt from worry now and again. "Who doesn't worry?"

"You could always retire," he suggested with a mischievous twinkle in those sexy eyes. "We could spend our mornings watching the world go by and our evenings admiring the sunset from anywhere in the world that pleases you."

She couldn't say his offer wasn't tempting, but Victoria understood that she would never be happy doing *only* that. Retirement was not for her. "I can't say that I haven't considered just that," she admitted. Especially since Lucas had stepped down from his high-powered position in D.C., choosing to serve as a consultant when needed and usually via a telephone conference. Once in a while, he still had to fly to the District to take care of highly classified business personally. Then there was the pending arrival of their first grandchild.

In spite of all those seemingly logical reasons to

choose retirement, she knew herself too well. "But you know that would never be enough."

"I would be shocked if you had proposed otherwise." Lucas leaned forward and gave a covert look around to ensure no one was within hearing distance. "Speaking of work, Mildred wanted me to give you a message."

Victoria lifted an eyebrow skeptically. "Did Mildred send you to bring me back?" She hadn't intended to stay this long; time had gotten away from her. It amused her immensely that Lucas didn't mind playing messenger. Just another indication of how very much he loved her.

"You had a call from a client she felt you wouldn't want to miss. The appointment is scheduled for half an hour from now."

Her calendar was clear this morning. An unexpected appointment wouldn't be a problem. "Who's the client?" Someone in a hurry, obviously. Someone who wanted to see her personally rather than one of the two men who served as her seconds-in-command.

"Desmond Van Valkenberg."

Surprised, she tried to remember the last time she'd had Mr. Van Valkenberg or his representative in her office. Three years? Four? A corporate profile request, if her memory served her correctly. She didn't know Desmond that well, but she had known his father quite well. Hershel Van Valkenberg had been a giant in finance, a man of his word until the day he passed away twelve years ago. He preferred doing business the old-fashioned way, himself and in person. His son had proved to be a vastly different businessman, with numerous representatives to see after his interests while he remained reclusive and as far from the limelight as possible.

"He's sending his representative, a Mr. Lance Brody, to see you."

Mr. Brody was his personal attorney, not one of the corporate team he usually sent. Victoria had met the gentleman once at a reception she had attended and where Van Valkenberg had made one of his rare appearances. Brody was a very formal man. He gave new meaning to the term stuffed shirt, but had quite the stellar reputation as an attorney.

In any event, she should prepare for his arrival. She stood. "Under the circumstances I suppose we should get back."

Lucas pushed to his feet with effort. Some days, the fact that he wore a prosthetic for a right leg was more pronounced than others. Her heart squeezed at the memory of how he'd gained that at times unwieldy appliance. His sacrifice as a prisoner of war had saved her first husband's life long, long ago. Lucas was not only a wonderful husband, he was also a man of unparalleled courage. He'd proven to be her savior more than once.

He offered his arm. "Shall we?"

Victoria looped her arm in his and thanked God again for this wondrous man. To have known and loved two great men in her lifetime was truly a blessing few had the good fortune of claiming. "Absolutely."

A few minutes later, Victoria sat in her office reviewing the Van Valkenberg file Mildred had already pulled for her convenience. The work the Colby Agency had done for this client, and for his father before him, generally involved background searches on potential employees and profiles of companies targeted for potential mergers. She had every reason to anticipate that the coming meeting would be more of the same. But she was puzzled that he had chosen to send his personal attorney.

A light rap on the door alerted her to Brody's arrival. Mildred opened the door and announced him. Victoria, though strangely preoccupied with her own thoughts this Monday morning, couldn't help noticing her longtime secretary's glow. Another weekend with her beau, she supposed. Victoria felt certain those two would be setting a wedding date soon. And why not? Life was too precious to waste.

Victoria rose from her chair. "Thank you, Mildred." She shifted her full attention to her visitor. "Mr. Brody, come in, please."

Lance Brody crossed the room in three long strides and, shifting his briefcase to his left hand, extended his right across her desk. "Mrs. Colby-Camp, it's a pleasure to see you again."

Victoria shook his hand, acknowledging his greeting with a nod. "Why don't we sit and you can tell me what it is that Mr. Van Valkenberg requires of my agency. We're anxious to be of service."

Brody sat, his shoulders as stiff as the freshly starched gray suit he wore. "Our needs are quite different this time I'm afraid. This time is…personal."

A new kind of tension rippled through Victoria. *Personal.* Desmond Van Valkenberg was not the kind of man who often allowed anyone outside his most intimate circle close enough to know his most personal business.

"I see. Why don't you start at the beginning and give me the details." Victoria settled into her chair and waited for the representative of her client to proceed as he saw fit.

Brody crossed his long legs and appeared to settle in. "Some ten years ago, a female companion of Mr. Van Valkenberg's, a Miss Ashley Orrick, gave birth to a son while living here in Chicago with him. The two had been involved for just over one year."

Victoria was surprised to hear this. She wasn't aware that Desmond had any children. "Was proof of paternity obtained?"

The lawyer nodded. "Certainly, but the trouble ultimately proved unnecessary. There were a few minor complications at birth and the child's blood type confirmed the truth of his parentage. Mr. Van Valkenberg has a very rare blood type. The child has the same."

"Has there been contact with the child or the mother recently?"

"Not since the child was about three months old. The woman, Miss Orrick, left abruptly and took the child with her."

The idea that Van Valkenberg would simply permit her to leave with his son in tow surprised Victoria. "Did Mr. Van Valkenberg attempt to stop her or to exercise his rights as the father at that time or since?"

"No," Brody explained carefully. "There were problems with the woman. She threatened to blackmail him, using the child as leverage. At one point, she went so far as to contact one of his rivals in an attempt to undermine an ongoing business deal." Brody shrugged. "Frankly, I'm convinced she was unbalanced. Her irrational behavior only worsened as time went by."

"And yet," Victoria interrupted, "you allowed her to leave with the child."

"Actually," he said pointedly, clearly somewhat offended by her suggestion, "she took the child and disappeared. *After* stealing a considerable sum of money from Mr. Van Valkenberg, I might add. This woman was a gold digger from the outset, I'm afraid."

"Mr. Van Valkenberg wishes to find the child now," Victoria guessed.

"Yes." Brody opened his briefcase and took out a file. He leaned forward and offered it to Victoria. "You'll find all the information we have on Miss Orrick in this file, including numerous photos, but, unfortunately, the photos are ten years old."

Victoria accepted the file, considered the contents a moment before asking, "Why now? After all these years?" She needed to know the rest of the story. The Colby Agency prided itself on discretion, both in the cases they accepted and in the way they conducted their investigations. However long Van Valkenberg had been a client, she needed clarification on exactly what he wanted and, equally important, why.

Mr. Brody leveled a solemn gaze at her. "As you're well aware, Mr. Van Valkenberg has always been a man dedicated to his work and inordinately reserved in his social agenda. He hasn't taken the time to develop or nurture any sort of real personal life. However, he recently learned news that has forced him to rethink his past decisions."

Victoria braced herself for what came next. Judging by the man's expression as well as his somber tone, the news was not good.

"Mr. Van Valkenberg has given permission for me to share this information with you, but, as you will see, the public cannot know, for obvious reasons. He's dying. According to the team of specialists working on his case, he has five or six months at best. He feels he has accomplished all that he'd set out to in the business world for a man barely forty. However, he knows that not acquainting himself with his only child would be a disgrace on a personal level. This is his greatest wish. We must locate the boy before it's too late."

Victoria understood how Mr. Van Valkenberg must feel. The thought of never seeing her son again had been almost too much to bear. She'd been down that path. No parent should ever have to feel that kind of pain and desolation.

Victoria made a decision then and there to do all she could to ensure that Desmond's son was found. "Mr. Brody, I would like you to convey to Mr. Van Valkenberg my personal feelings of regret for this untimely tragedy. Assure him that we at the Colby Agency will do all within our power to find his son and, as always, with the utmost discretion."

Mr. Brody acknowledged her words with a nod. "I will relay your assurances, but Mr. Van Valkenberg has no doubt where your agency is concerned. I would, however, like to give him some sense of the time frame you feel you require to accomplish your work, since time is clearly of the essence."

Victoria thought about her answer for a moment. She didn't want to sound overly optimistic since the woman and child had been missing for ten years, but, at the same time, she didn't want to worry her client needlessly.

"One week minimum," she allowed. "I wouldn't expect, barring any unforeseen circumstances, more than two. It's much more difficult for a woman to hide with a child in tow."

"Excellent." Mr. Brody stood and extended his hand. "We will look forward to hearing from you, Mrs. Colby-Camp."

Victoria rose as well, shook his hand once more and gave final assurances that Mr. Van Valkenberg needn't worry. The Colby agency was on the case.

When Brody had left, Victoria again considered the file he'd provided. Ashley Orrick, according to the documents in the file, had been twenty-one at the time she'd given birth. Very young. Strawberry blond hair, pale skin with a scattering of delicate freckles, and green eyes, all of which she could have easily changed with hair color, contacts and sufficient makeup.

Miss Orrick had grown up in a small farming community in Indiana. Her father had passed away when she was eighteen but her mother still lived on the small family farm.

The fact that she had a surviving family member would most likely make the job of finding her somewhat less difficult. Victoria turned over the picture of the missing woman's mother to find a note scribbled on the back: Uncooperative. Combative.

A good deal of background information had been gathered by Brody himself, it appeared. Ashley had attended the local high school and gone on to attend a nearby university. After graduating from college, she'd come to Chicago and met Desmond at a job fair in one of his uncommon public appearances.

She hadn't gotten a job, but she had moved in with him within two months. One year later, she disappeared after a Mommy and Baby Yoga class.

The child, in his three-month-old photo and in the physical description listed in Brody's report, appeared to have his father's coloring, dark hair and olive skin. Too early to tell about the eyes—dark, perhaps brown if the color remained the same.

Victoria summoned Mildred on the intercom. "Would you have Ben and Keith come to my office please."

Ben Haygood was the agency's top systems man. He could do just about anything with a computer. His resourcefulness with gadgets was unparalleled.

Keith Devers had worked for the agency for several years in the research department. Only recently had he agreed to Victoria's prodding and moved into investigations. He was more than qualified for the position of investigator but he'd hesitated for some time, preferring to delve into research from his desk rather than to move into the field.

Victoria found Keith's shyness quite refreshing.

She recognized that he would blossom into a terrific investigator once he got his feet wet. All he needed was a little prompting and the right case. He'd shadowed a couple of other cases already. This one would serve quite well for putting him out there for his first solo. A simple missing person case with no real theatrics attached. With one or two cases this uncomplicated under his belt, he'd be ready for something with a little more drama.

Keith arrived just then. "You wanted to see me?"

"Yes, come in, Keith."

Ben poked his head through the door next, his glasses as well as his tie askew as usual. "Did you call for me, Victoria?"

"I did. Please join us, Ben."

Ben half stumbled through the open door as if her answer had startled him, then took a moment to right his eyewear and straighten his tie. Victoria kept her amusement tucked out of sight, though it wasn't easy. Ben's clothes were a bit rumpled, and he wore his typical, perpetually distracted expression. The quintessential computer geek. Extremely intelligent with absolutely no fashion sense or social grace.

Keith, however, was the other end of the spectrum. Elegantly dressed, meticulous manners. The man was a study in social etiquette. And equally intelligent.

"Crashing the system was a necessary risk," Ben said the moment he stopped in front of her desk. His posture resembled that of a soldier's while standing at attention before a superior officer. "It was inevitable in order to accomplish the download."

Uncertain she wanted to know what his announcement meant, she ventured, "A systems crash?"

He held up both hands as if to stop any further conclusions on her part. "Nothing to worry about, Victoria. Things were back up and running by 2 a.m. Not a problem. I knew what I was doing."

She smiled. "I'm certain of that, Ben." She looked from him to Keith. "Please have a seat, gentlemen."

When both men, each as different from the other as a glass of cola and a glass of champagne, had laid claim to wingback chairs facing her desk, Victoria began, "We have a new case that I believe is the one that should launch your investigative career, Keith."

He tensed visibly. "Great." But his deep voice failed to relay the word with any enthusiasm. He smoothed a hand down the length of his striped tie. "When do I start?"

"As soon as we have some of the preliminary details out of the way." She shifted her attention to Ben. "That's where you come in, Ben. We'll need a computer age progression on this photo." She passed the picture of the baby to him. "And one on the mother, as well."

Ben scratched his head as he studied the ten-year-old photographs. "The female won't be a problem.

But you know the process works a lot better if the kid is at least two years old." Concern spelled itself out in his expression. "I can't make any promises about real accuracy with an infant."

"Do your best." She hoped that would make him feel more at ease, she should have known better.

He studied the photo again and his right leg started to bounce nervously. "I have a friend in…" He shrugged, looked embarrassed. "Well, it doesn't matter where he works. He has access to this state-of-the-art process that's not available to us regular folks. I might be able to get him to do this one as a favor to me."

There was the Ben Victoria knew and loved. He always found a way to get things done. How had he worked in the bowels of research so long without her notice? The answer was easy; he hadn't wanted to be noticed. That he had been a few months ago was an accident. He'd discovered a flaw in one of the agency's computer security processes and had spoken up. It wasn't until then that anyone had any idea about his genius. And that's what it was—pure genius.

"That would be wonderful, Ben. We need to find this child. Time is our enemy."

"Is the child ill?" Keith wanted to know.

"No." Victoria gave the folder with the rest of its contents to him. "The biological father is terminally ill and he wishes to know his son before he dies. The mother left when the child was only three months old and she hasn't been heard from since."

As he reviewed the contents of the folder, Keith asked, "Are we sure she's still alive?"

Victoria had read the file reports on where Brody had looked for the woman. He hadn't found anything that indicated she was deceased, but then he wasn't experienced in the art of finding missing people, either.

"We can't be sure, but we need to find out as quickly as possible. Our client only has a few short months to live. Since the Van Valkenberg family has been a client of this agency for a number of years, I'm putting my best on the case."

Keith's gaze collided with hers. "Victoria, are you sure it's me you want on this one?"

Again, his uneasiness was evident. "Very sure," she confirmed.

Ben jumped up. "If you don't need me for anything else, I'd like to get started on this."

"Please do. The moment you hear from your friend, you should forward the results to Keith."

Ben nodded. "Will do."

He hurried out of the office, the fire obviously burning in his belly to accomplish his mission. Just another thing Victoria appreciated about him. He loved his work and appeared to relish a challenge.

Her attention came back to rest on Keith's blond head bowed over the file. Such a handsome young man. Blond hair, blue eyes, and well tanned from running five miles every morning beneath the July sun. What was it that made such a good-looking, intelligent young man so unsure of himself? He'd graduated at the top of his university class back in Nebraska. He'd come to Chicago, gone to work for the *Tribune* in the research department and done well.

His seemingly abrupt decision to move yet again, this time from journalism to private investigations, had seemed odd when she'd first interviewed him more than two years ago. But his résumé had been impeccable and highly attractive to any potential employer. She hadn't questioned her good fortune too closely. Keith Devers was an asset, the Colby Agency was glad to have him on board.

Perhaps she'd grown cynical in the past few years, always looking for the underlying motivation in all things. She did wonder, however, how such a handsome young man had stayed unattached until the ripe old age of thirty-two.

Maybe he was also shy in his personal life. Certainly there were no known skeletons in his closet. The man had never been in trouble in his life. Not even a parking ticket. And in Chicago, that was saying something.

He looked up then and asked, "So, I'm supposed to find her and the boy and bring them back to Chicago?"

"That would be the optimum scenario," she

allowed, knowing from experience that it would never be that easy.

"What if she doesn't want to come back?"

The blunt question was nothing she hadn't expected.

"Then we'll take our client to her."

Chapter Two

Thank God the sun had started to set. Still, it was damned hot.

Keith sat in a car outside the Orrick family home in a small farming community less than an hour outside South Bend. The modest home sat amid several hundred acres of farmland that had slowly been sold off over the past ten years. Newer homes had popped up on most of the parcels sold, leaving the Orrick home a lonely relic of the past separated by scarcely ten acres from the new, bigger and better models.

A thorough background search had shown that Ashley Orrick's mother, Mary, lived alone since her husband's death fifteen years ago and her daughter's departure for college shortly after that. He'd checked the land line records associated with the address and saw that no calls had come from outside the local calling area. According to Keith's research, Mrs. Orrick did not own a cellular phone, but that didn't mean she didn't have one. Ben had equipped Keith for that scenario.

Keith had considered at length his limited options on how to approach the older woman and decided that an extreme cover story was necessary. Outright lying wasn't one of his favorite tactics, but under the circumstances it was, unfortunately, necessary. No way would the mother willingly give up her daughter's location. He felt certain she wouldn't even talk to him unless he gave her a hell of an excuse.

Technically, he wasn't outright lying, but it felt entirely too much like deceit to sit right with his conscience. The offer was legitimate; it just somehow felt wrong. Maybe it was because Keith suspected Van Valkenberg would take legal action to ensure Ashley Orrick didn't elude him again quicker than she could cash the check for back child support.

On the other side of the coin was Desmond Van Valkenberg. He had a right to know his son. Ashley Orrick had taken that right from him ten years ago. She'd used a number of means of deceit, including taking on one or more identities to do so. Keith shouldn't feel guilty…but he did.

Shoving aside the undermining emotion, he emerged from his car and reached into the back seat for his briefcase. At least he would learn one thing about Miss Ashley Orrick at the end of this exercise: her price.

If she were a gold digger as Brody claimed, she would have a price. In Keith's opinion, she certainly hadn't behaved like someone out for the money, but he would reserve judgment until he had all the facts.

He walked up the dusty sidewalk. July's lack of rain ensured dying grass and rising utility costs if one wanted to stay cool. Though Mrs. Mary Orrick's home didn't have the convenience of central air-conditioning, an individual unit droned monotonously in a window on the side of the house. A steady drizzle of water dripped from its rusty housing. Even with the sun dropping behind the trees in the distance, he already missed the cool air that had been circulating in his vehicle.

The shade on the porch provided some relief as he knocked on the screen door. He couldn't hear any sounds inside over the buzz of the air conditioner. An old pickup truck sat near the house; to his knowledge, Mrs. Orrick didn't own any other means of transportation, not even a tractor. All farm equipment had been sold off in the past decade.

The frame house looked badly in need of a paint job, possibly indicating the owner's inability to afford proper maintenance despite selling off her assets. He kicked aside the sympathy that immediately filtered into his thoughts. He had to remain objective. Not that he couldn't feel compassion for others, but before he allowed it to color his judgment, he needed all the facts.

A twist of the doorknob drew his attention. The door cracked open just far enough for the home's occupant to peek outside. "I don't go to church and I don't buy goods sold across a threshold. So don't waste your time or mine."

"Hello, Mrs. Orrick. My name is Keith Devers."

The narrow opening widened slightly to facilitate a better visual inspection. Eagle eyes surveyed him carefully. "What do you want?"

"I have a financial opportunity you need to be aware of." He patted his briefcase. "If I may come in and speak privately with you."

"I don't have any more land to sell."

Her voice told him to go, but the glint of hope in her eyes offered a different story. "Mrs. Orrick, this isn't about your land." He reminded himself not to let sympathy get in the way. Lots of folks in the farming business had suffered hard times. This wasn't about that. This was about a man who had every right to know his son. "This is a far more lucrative offer."

She gave him a final once-over, then opened the door. "Just remember, I'm not buying anything."

Across the threshold, with the door closed behind him, Keith felt his confidence level rise. All he had to do now was convince this lady that reuniting father and son would be in everyone's best interests. And, in fact, Keith did have a nice offer from Van Valkenberg. Van Valkenberg felt compelled to pay that back child support, which amounted to a sizable, inordinately generous sum. A small fortune, in fact. Enough to satisfy the financial needs of both Orrick women. Allowing the child to know his father would benefit everyone involved.

"Sit if you like," Mary Orrick offered as she took what was clearly her favorite chair, an upholstered rocker that looked well worn and sported a cozy doily on each wood-trimmed arm.

He settled onto the sofa and placed his briefcase on the coffee table. When he leaned forward to open it, she said, "Before you go to any trouble, what's he paying you?"

Keith stilled. "Excuse me?"

"That monster Van Valkenberg. What's he paying you to try to find my daughter?"

Several strands of gray hair had slipped from the clasp holding her hair at the nape of her neck. Decades of hard work under the brutal sun had aged her skin well beyond her years. She looked tired and impatient, yet a keen intelligence shone through that depleted veneer.

Keith straightened, kept his gaze steady on hers. "Mr. Van Valkenberg's attorney has retained the services of my agency to attempt to locate his son. There are hefty back payments of child support as well as estate issues that need to be settled. Your grandson is Mr. Van Valkenberg's only heir."

Mrs. Orrick's gaze tapered suspiciously. "Are you saying his estate needs settling? Is he dead?"

This was where things got sticky. "I'm afraid I'm not at liberty to discuss that particular matter. I do have documents—" he reached for his briefcase again "—that provide for your grandson's financial future and the back payments I mentioned."

Keith passed the legal documents assigning Avery Van Valkenberg—the child's name on his birth certificate—sole beneficiary of Desmond Van Valkenberg's estate. Another document outlined payment of an appropriate amount of accumulated child support. As uncomfortable as Keith felt allowing the woman to believe that Van Valkenberg was practically dead already, the papers were legitimate. The kid would be incredibly rich very soon. And the guy was dying.

Mary Orrick studied the papers for a few moments, especially the final pages with Van Valkenberg's notarized signature. In time she looked up. "You leave these with me, Mr. Devers, as well as your business card and I'll see what I can do."

Combative? Uncooperative? Didn't make sense to Keith. The woman appeared quite reasonable and he was sure this wasn't the first time money had been offered for information leading to her daughter's whereabouts. Then again, he doubted anyone had ever let her believe the monster, as she had called him, was dead.

Keith gave her his card. "Use my cell number. I'm staying in a hotel in South Bend."

She looked at the card, raised skeptical eyebrows at him. "I'm not making any promises. We'll see is all I'm saying."

Keith left it at that. He'd accomplished the first stage of his plan. The next move was up to Mrs. Orrick and her daughter.

Outside, dusk had brought with it a noticeable drop in the temperature. He got into his car, turned around and drove down the long drive, away from the farmhouse in need of seemingly endless repairs.

Careful not to get out of range of Ben's latest gadget, he parked a short distance up the country road that served as the main route into this part of the county. He checked the settings, tucked the earpiece into place and waited for Mary Orrick to do what any mother would.

Less than ten minutes after Keith had left the house, someone inside, Mary Orrick no doubt, placed a call on a cellular phone. Three rings later, a soft female voice answered. "Hello."

"They sent someone new this time."

Silence.

Keith analyzed the one word the other female had uttered in greeting. He couldn't conclude with certainty that the woman was Ashley Orrick since he didn't have a voice pattern with which to compare it, but his instincts were leaning that way. He watched as the small screen on the handheld computer relayed the signal to one of Ben's contacts. All he needed was ninety seconds and that same contact would triangulate the exact location of the woman Mrs. Orrick had called.

Thank you, Ben.

"Not Brody?"

Again Keith played the cautiously chosen words over and over, committed each nuance of sound to memory. In his opinion, there was now no question about the woman's identity.

"No," Mary Orrick said. "A Keith Devers. He's from some private investigations agency in Chicago. He brought papers showing a high six-figure number Van Valkenberg's people are ready to pay in back child support, if you can believe that. But the real kicker he delivered is the *estate* papers. I think maybe Van Valkenberg's dead or on his deathbed."

"He can't be dead, Mother. It would have been in the papers."

Mother. Definitely Ashley.

"Come on," Keith muttered as he watched the small LCD screen. "Give me a location."

"True. But I'm looking at these papers. They name Jamie as the sole heir to his estate."

Jamie. She'd changed the boy's name.

"This could be a trap."

"I know," Mary relented with an audible sigh. "But I had to tell you, honey. This could mean your freedom and Jamie's is close at hand."

Keith tensed. Freedom? What the hell did that mean? He knew the two women likely hated the guy, but damn, wishing him dead was cold.

A series of high-pitched tones alerted him that the location had been acquired. South Bend? It couldn't be that simple. No way.

"Send me the papers the usual way. I'll take a look and we'll go from there."

The two exchanged good-byes wrought with palpable emotion. Keith jerked out the earpiece and focused on driving. He could be at the address in forty minutes. He hoped like hell she would still be there.

How could she have been living that close all this time and not have been discovered by Van Valkenberg's people? It didn't make sense. Brody didn't appear incompetent by any means.

Keith would know soon.

Forty-five minutes later, Keith sat outside a twenty-four-hour diner in South Bend.

"This can't be right," he murmured. Would Ashley Orrick have the nerve to work in the open in a place like this?

Keith had a very bad feeling that something was way out of sync here.

He got out of his car and surveyed the crowded

parking lot. Every instinct warned that solving this case wasn't going to be anywhere near this easy. But the location was all he had.

Floor-to-ceiling windows made up the length of the front facade of the diner. Booths, tables and even the long counter fronted by bar stools looked to be occupied. Four waitresses weaved around the maze of customers. Not one looked like his target, but all looked harried.

Since he knew this wasn't the only restaurant in town, he could only assume, judging by the crowd, that the food must be above average. But it wasn't the food he was interested in.

As he moved inside, he pretended to scour the place for an open table or stool, surveying each waitress a little more closely. Nope. Not one matched Ashley Orrick's description. That didn't mean she wasn't in the back working in the kitchen in some capacity. For that matter, she could be here having dinner. Just in case, he scanned the faces of customers a bit more slowly. No one caught his eye.

Noting the arrow pointing to a side corridor and the location of the restrooms, Keith made his way through the diner. He bypassed the men's room and took a chance. He knocked on the door of the ladies' room. When no one answered, he stuck his head inside and checked the stalls. Empty.

With a quick glance toward the diner to make sure no one was headed that way, he moved past the restrooms and the emergency rear exit, to the door marked Employees Only. He pushed into the kitchen and had just enough time to scrutinize the crew scrambling to fill orders before anyone noticed his presence and realized he didn't have any business poking his head through the door.

"Hey!" A short, stout woman shouted. "You can't be back here!"

"Sorry." He shrugged, tried to look embarrassed. "Bathroom?"

"The door marked Men's Room," another woman said with a smirk.

"Thanks," he mumbled, then quickly made his exit amid a rumble of laughter.

He returned to the dining room, located an unoccupied bar stool and made himself comfortable.

"You ready to order?"

He glanced up at the waitress waiting on the other side of the counter. A bottle blonde, tall, slim. Looked as if she'd worked one shift too many.

"Coffee." He pushed a smile into place, glanced at her nametag. Gina. When he was just a kid, his mom had been a waitress. Honest work, he remembered her saying. Honest but hard. As an adult he'd always left big tips.

"Cream? Sugar?" She had shored up a faint smile

in answer to his, but it appeared as mechanical as her one-word queries.

He shook his head. "Black."

"Anything else?"

"Nothing else."

A few moments later, she set the mug of steaming coffee in front of him and moved on to the next customer. As he savored the coffee, he watched the patrons coming and going.

Half an hour passed and still no sign of anyone even remotely matching Ashley Orrick's description. He'd considered numerous possibilities. Had she dyed her hair? Blond? Brunette? What about her eyes? Would she be wearing colored contacts to camouflage her vivid green eyes? He had to admit he'd never known anyone with eyes that brilliant. They shone like jewels. That sounded cheesy, but it was true. He'd definitely know those eyes if he spotted them, even in a crowd and from a reasonable distance.

She could have gained weight. Lost weight, though not much if she wanted to maintain her health. Ten years ago, she'd looked thin enough.

Ben had done an age progression on her and estimated that she wouldn't look that different unless she'd had a significant weight change or suffered from an illness or been in an accident that altered her physical appearance. He'd gotten the age progression on the infant, as well. And though Ben's friend, who Keith suspected worked for Homeland Security, asserted that the progression was ninety percent accurate, Keith would have to see the kid to believe it.

Still, he paid attention to every male child and each female adult who entered or exited the diner.

And nothing.

Not an hour later.

Not two hours later.

He'd been had.

"HE'S HERE. Been hanging out a couple of hours."

Ashley felt her heart thump against her sternum. Damn. She should have known the story this guy had given her mother was too good to be true.

"You're sure it's him?"

"Yep. I'm looking right at him. He's wearing that navy suit your mother described. The white shirt and red tie. He's tall, blond hair, great blue eyes. Tanned. Just like one of those surfer guys. Damned good-looking for a cop."

"Not a cop. A P.I."

"Whatever."

Ashley closed her eyes and exhaled a weary breath. When would it end? When would she and Jamie have a normal life? *Never,* said her heart.

"Can you pix him for me?"

"Sure."

"And Gina," Ashley went on, a new kind of fear suddenly kindling inside her.

"Yeah?"

"Be careful. I don't know…" What was it? Nothing she could name or put her finger on. "Something about this one scares me." Maybe it was the enormity of the offer Desmond had thrown on the table this time. She sensed a desperation in the act she'd never felt before.

"Don't worry, Ash, I've got this dude's number. Soon as I hang up, I'll send you a snap of him."

"Thanks, Gina."

Ashley hung up her cell phone. The one she used to contact only Gina. She had three altogether. One for calling her mother, which bounced all over the country, ultimately showing that the call originated from Delta's Diner in South Bend. And then the one she used for calling her son.

She blinked back the emotion that burned in her eyes when she thought of her precious boy. It had been two weeks since she'd seen him. It got harder and harder every time she had to leave him.

When he'd been just a small child, it had been easier. He'd cried. She'd cried. But she had known that he really didn't understand what was happening and that he would love her and forgive her; the fact that she'd left him would be forgotten by the next time she came to see him.

Things were different now. He was ten. He no longer cried, he asked questions. Demanded answers. He no longer forgave her so easily when she left and then returned sometimes days, sometimes weeks later.

It was hell.

She squeezed her eyes shut but failed to block a few of the tears that would not be contained. She hated Desmond Van Valkenberg.

Why didn't he just leave them alone?

At first, it had been about the threats. If she ever told anyone what she knew…what she'd seen…

But she'd never told a soul. And he'd left her alone.

Then, after two years, as if he'd suspected she had told his secrets, he'd shown up in her life again. She and Jamie had barely escaped him.

It was several days before she understood why he'd appeared in her life once more. The remains of one of the women with whom he'd carried on one of his many kinky affairs had been discovered. Her face had been plastered all over the news and the papers. Ashley couldn't remember her having gone missing, but then she'd been busy trying to elude Desmond at the time.

It wasn't until those remains had been found that Ashley had known exactly what Desmond was capable of.

Murder.

Her decision to take her son and disappear so

completely that she scarcely knew herself anymore had definitely been the right one.

Even now, eight years after the remains had been found, the case had not been solved.

Nothing about the case had connected the dead woman to Desmond. Nothing likely would. He had the kind of money that could cover up any injustice.

But she had the videotape.

The single piece of evidence that could prove he'd had a dangerous affair with the woman right before she went missing. That didn't make him her killer, though the brutality of the sex they shared had been damned frightening. It would, however, make him a suspect. He wouldn't stand for that. The extent that he appeared to be willing to go to in order to see that the tape never got into the hands of the authorities was the single most compelling reason for Ashley to be scared.

She hadn't realized the significance of the tape she'd taken from among dozens upon dozens she'd discovered after her son was born. No, taking that particular tape hadn't amounted to brilliance or even luck. She'd merely taken the one that showcased her as one of Desmond's conquests.

She shuddered when she let the memories emerge from that place where she'd locked them away so long ago.

Desmond Van Valkenberg was capable of anything. *Anything.*

She'd run with her child in tow to protect him from the evil his father craved. Besides, Desmond didn't like baggage. He'd been fascinated by Ashley. That was the only reason he'd allowed her to actually live with him for more than a year. Her foolish vulnerability had enticed him. Even the child they'd created together had amused him for a time.

But that hadn't lasted very long.

She'd realized it was time to go the night he'd tried to kill her.

Her cell phone rang and she jumped. She glanced around the store to make sure no one had come in to witness her foolish behavior. She had to get a grip here.

Pressing her hand to her chest she sucked in breath. Stay calm. Being calm and rational was her only defense against Desmond. She had to be smarter than him. Quicker on her feet.

He'd left her alone for a very long time now. What was the reason for his sudden renewed interest?

There had to be some motivation for his trouble. Had the investigation into that old case been resurrected?

Had he killed another of his consorts? She hadn't seen anything in the news related to that sort of case in the Chicago area. There were only three other women on the tape besides her. One was dead. It wouldn't be difficult to determine if the other two were alive and well. Maybe she should look into that possibility.

She opened her phone to view the picture Gina had just sent her via her own camera phone.

The image of the man her mother had described filled the small screen.

Ashley moistened her lips and told her heart to calm. Young, she decided. Maybe her age or younger. Handsome. He looked…harmless.

But he wouldn't be.

Desmond Van Valkenberg had sent him.

Nothing about Desmond could be considered harmless, most assuredly not his hired help.

Whatever he was after, she had to make sure he didn't find Jamie.

She had to protect her son at all costs.

She sat down on the stool behind the counter and stared at the image on her phone's tiny screen.

Her intuition nudged her, warned her, that this time she wouldn't escape so easily. This guy looked as determined as he did handsome.

She closed the phone and looked up as the bell over the store's entrance door jingled. A familiar face strolled into the convenience store.

"Evening, Mr. Talley, how are you tonight?" Somehow she managed to sound chipper when she felt anything but.

He grunted from beneath the bill of his cap. "Can you believe I had to come out for milk at this hour?" He shook his head and shuffled toward the cooler at the back of the store. "I swear. Couldn't she have noticed that we were out before bedtime?"

Ashley had to smile. The man was one of her regular customers and the *she* he spoke of was his wife. They'd been married forty years and he never let anyone forget it. For all his grumbling, Ashley knew he worshiped the ground his wife walked on.

"Thank the Lord for all-night convenience stores," he groused as he plopped the gallon of milk onto the counter. "How's your night going, Nola?"

That was her name now. Nola Childress. Nola who lived and worked in Waynesville, Missouri. A nobody in the middle of nowhere.

"Like all the rest, Mr. Talley. Quiet." That was another way she stayed out of the mainstream. She worked the graveyard shift.

That was her life. Nobody, nowhere, nightshift.

Not even her own mother knew where she was.

Whatever Mr. Keith Devers's agenda was, he couldn't know, either.

That was the one hard and fast rule she lived by. Every instinct warned her that it was the sole reason she and her son were both still alive.

Chapter Three

Keith admitted defeat at midnight. Fifteen minutes later he'd shed his shoes, jacket and tie and fallen across the bed in his hotel room.

He stared at his cell phone. He'd called Ben to find out what the hell had gone wrong with the trace, but the jury was still out on that issue. Ben had spouted off a couple of possibilities; both flew right over Keith's head. Fact was, he didn't really care what happened; he just didn't want it to happen again and he needed to know the location from which Ashley Orrick had called. Now. This minute, no later than the next.

Was that too much to ask?

He blew out a disgusted breath. Things weren't supposed to go this way. His first case in the field and problems were cropping up already.

Definitely not cool.

Hopefully he could make up for lost time tomorrow.

He'd researched Ashley Orrick's past every which way possible. There wasn't a damned iota of information on the woman or the child newer than eight years ago. Both had disappeared, seemingly fallen off the planet.

Yet, logic dictated that they were somewhere. Pure physics. Matter occupied space and all that jazz. All he had to do was flush the woman out of hiding and finding the kid would be a piece of cake after that. Chances were wherever Mommy went, the little boy went, too.

The question was, why hide the kid from his rich daddy? Was she afraid of the consequences of her actions ten years ago? She'd taken the money and ran. Big deal. Even if Van Valkenberg were of the mind to press charges, the statute of limitations had likely run out on her alleged crime.

What was she running from? The boy was Van Valkenberg's biological child. Van Valkenberg was worth megamillions. Why walk away from that kind of security? Didn't sound like gold digger tactics.

It didn't make sense at all. If she was the scam artist, why ditch such a bountiful source of dough? She had the platinum card with the unlimited credit limit in that kid.

Keith shoved his fingers through his hair. He needed sleep. He would be able to think better after a few hours of shuteye. Maybe by then he'd hear from Ben with something on how the Orrick woman overrode the trace on the call her mother had made to her.

Maybe she was smarter than Van Valkenberg and his people had estimated. She was definitely cagier than Keith had anticipated.

He closed his eyes and tuned out the questions one by one. No more thinking. A few hours' sleep would give him the clear head he needed for determining his next course of action.

The chirp of his cell phone disrupted the silence.

Keith sat up and blinked twice before the numbers on the clock became clear: 1:30 a.m. He grabbed the phone off the bedside table.

"Devers."

"I think I've got it."

Ben.

Keith scrubbed a hand over his face. "I'm listening."

"You see, she piggybacked her number on several others, bouncing around the Midwest ending up in South Bend. The technology isn't anything new, but your average Joe, or Betty in this case, wouldn't know about it. Not that it's a problem to find it." He laughed. "The needed gadgets are available right on the Internet. But her one mistake was in her post office box."

"Her post office box?" Keith's brow furrowed in confusion as he started to button his shirt. Somehow the conversation had jumped from cell phones to post office boxes and he didn't quite follow. Maybe that hour of sleep had been just enough to ensure his brain staged a rebellion against waking up.

"Yeah. You see, you have to have a billing address. No billing address, no cell phone. Unless, of course, you're using the pay-as-you-go kind and she isn't. So, she used an alias and a post office box."

Keith was just about to tell him to get to the point, when he went on, "Only problem is, when I hacked into the files—" Ben cleared his throat "—well, actually I had a contact who did the hacking. Anyway, she listed her physical residence. It's required, like I said. Once I had that, I cross-refer-enced with the DMV. It's her, all right. The hair's dif-ferent. The eyes, too, but there's no question that Ashley Orrick is one and the same as Nola Childress.

"I don't get it," Ben said, sounding surprised or maybe a little disappointed his prey had fallen down on the point. "All she would have had to do was use someone else's address. Simple. I'll bet she—"

"Where is she, Ben?" Keith stood and shoved his feet into his shoes.

"Oh…ah…she's in Waynesville, Missouri. You could be there by 7 a.m. if you leave now. I projec-ted a route to her home address, calculated the distance and driving time. I sent it to your pocket PC."

"Thanks, Ben."

Keith closed his phone; otherwise, his colleague

might go on forever. He did love to talk about gadgets and such. Keith glanced at the clock again. One hour's sleep was better than none. He reached for his jacket and tie, surveyed the room to ensure he hadn't forgotten anything and left.

In the car, he dragged the pocket PC from his jacket, downloaded and checked his final destination.

He had to admit she'd picked an excellent place to get lost.

But he had something she didn't—Ben Haygood.

ASHLEY FORCED the orange juice past her lips. Her stomach quivered traitorously but she made herself drink for Jamie's sake.

He carefully sat his juice glass on the table. "How long can you stay?"

She pushed a smile into place. "Just for today." Her lips trembled in spite of her best efforts. God, she hated this.

He averted his dark gaze, choosing to stare at his uneaten eggs rather than his mother. He didn't have to say anything. Ashley knew exactly what he was thinking. His mother's visits grew farther and farther apart. Her excuses for the long absences were less and less creative. Each time it was more difficult to fool her extremely intelligent son. Pain twisted in her chest. How could she keep doing this to him?

But how could she risk otherwise?

"What would you like to do?" She pushed aside her untouched plate and clasped her hands atop the table. "You name it, baby, and we'll spend the day making it happen. Just you and me."

"I'm not a baby."

Oh, yeah, she'd forgotten that. Ten-year-old boys didn't like being called babies. "Sorry."

He picked at his eggs. "I have chores."

Ashley closed her eyes to hold back an onslaught of emotion. This wasn't his fault. She couldn't let him see how much his response hurt.

Since he'd started school, she'd left him in the care of her dear friend Marla Beck. Ashley had gone to elementary school with Marla, but they hadn't seen each other since sixth grade. Ashley would always believe that God had led her to Springfield and back into Marla's life. Marla had two small girls of her own, but she'd opened her home to Jamie in order to give him some much needed stability. Ashley couldn't count on staying in one place long enough to facilitate his education. Dragging him around from school to school would only send up a red flag for anyone searching for the two of them. Leaving him with Marla was the hardest thing she'd ever had to do, but it was the right thing to do.

Marla gave Jamie what she couldn't. That thought tightened in her chest, pressed in around her heart. It was true. Here, in Marla's home, he had the guarantee of waking up in the same bed each morning. A good school where he could bond with other boys and girls his age and develop lifelong friendships. Church on Sunday morning. All the right things a kid needed to grow up emotionally healthy and physically strong.

Ashley's friend refused payment for her kindness. She accepted only what it took to keep Jamie in clothes and other necessary school or medical expenses. She was truly a fine person. She'd lost her husband to an automobile accident several years ago, but he'd left her financially secure, enabling her to be a stay-at-home mom. Marla insisted this was the least she could do for Jamie and Ashley. Ashley was pretty sure it had more to do with how much she cared for Jamie than anything else. Ashley and Marla wanted their children to have the same kind of happy childhood they'd both enjoyed.

"I could help you do your chores first," Ashley offered. She wanted to grab him and hold him close. To beg him to forgive her for the mistakes she'd made. To plead with him to love her the way he used to when a few hugs and kisses could make up for most anything. But first and foremost, she had to respect his feelings. This couldn't be about her.

He shrugged. "I guess that'd be okay."

"All right!" She couldn't hide her excitement.

"First, we have to clean up the table." He said this with the slightest glimmer of enthusiasm.

"Okay." She hoped he didn't hear the quiver of her voice in that one word. It hurt so bad to watch him hold back like this…afraid to love his own mother. Afraid to count on her the way a child should be able to count on his parent.

She helped her son scrape the plates and put them in the dishwasher, along with their glasses and silverware. They wiped the table together and checked to make sure nothing had been forgotten, such as leaving the milk on the counter.

"Now what?" She looked to him for direction. Let him lead.

"I have to make my bed." He scratched his head. "I forgot that earlier. Ms. Marla told me you were here and I…forgot."

Ashley's heart leapt. He'd heard she was here and he'd gotten excited enough to forget part of his routine. Maybe there was hope for them after all.

"I'm pretty handy at making beds."

He nodded. "I remember."

Her heart so heavy she could scarcely breathe, she followed her son up the stairs to the room Marla had kindly decorated in a NASCAR theme just for him. Together, they made the bed and tidied his room.

He showed her his newest models. The tedious work of putting together the model cars was his favorite hobby. While some kids played their video games and watched endless hours of television,

Jamie would rather build models than eat when he was hungry. Maybe getting lost in the exacting work was his way of dealing with the hit-and-run visits of his mother.

When he'd finished showing off his latest handiwork, Jamie looked up at his mom and said, "You wanna see my final report card?"

She'd forgotten to look at it last time. He'd told her all about it, but she'd had to go before they'd gotten around to reviewing it together the way they usually did. She'd felt immensely guilty about that. He hadn't mentioned it again when she'd called him night after night or even when she'd returned for a day here and there. His silence told her how disappointed he was. Though school had been out for more than a month, the oversight obviously still nagged at him.

They sat on the bed, side by side, and he went over each subject, reciting what he liked about it and what he didn't. Whatever his preference, he always kept an A average.

Ashley felt her spirits soar as she listened to her son talk about the girl who'd chased after him the last couple of weeks of school. Thankfully, he hadn't had any trouble with bullies this year. Maybe that talk they'd had about him standing up for himself had done the trick. He'd listened well and done a great job handling any situation that arose without crossing the line into the same sort of aggressive behavior himself.

Something inside Ashley stilled, withered just a little as her eyes roved over the final section of the report card with her son's name on it. At the end of each reporting period in the space indicated for the parent's signature, Marla had signed her name.

Of course she had. She was Jamie's legal guardian.

Ashley had known this particular task would fall under her friend's duties. As were so many other everyday, little things that many mothers took for granted.

Like checking behind his ears after he bathed. Or ensuring that his homework was done. Tucking him in at night. All the things she used to do.

Needing to get past the moment she ruffled his hair, the way she used to when he was about five. He ducked away. But she understood the gesture wasn't about her touch. Her child was growing up on her. And she was missing most of it.

"I think such a stellar report card deserves a really special treat. What do you say we go to Brewster's and have one of their triple-decker ice cream cones?"

His face turned serious, that dark gaze settling fully on hers. "Do you have to leave today? Can't you stay just one night?"

This was the moment she had dreaded even before she'd arrived at Marla's home. Knowing that question would come had haunted her the entire trip from Waynesville to Springfield.

"You know I'd give anything to stay," she offered softly, struggling to keep her voice even. "But it's too risky. The bad men could find you and then they'd take you away and I might never see you again." She'd told him this story a million times. The idea had always terrified him, but not nearly as much as it terrified her. She knew too well just how true it was.

"Sometimes I think I'm never going to see you again anyway." His gaze dropped to his lap where his hands rested as if he didn't quite know what to do with them. "It feels like forever when you're gone."

The bottom dropped out of Ashley's stomach, leaving an emptiness that instantly began to swell with crushing intensity. "You're safe with Marla, Jamie. As much as I miss you, I'm willing to sacrifice my own feelings to ensure you're always safe."

His eyes locked with hers once more. "What about my feelings? What if I want things to be the way they used to be? I don't care about the bad men. I just want to be with you."

The crack in her heart widened, sending a searing pain through her that took her breath away. "I know, sweetie. But we have to be very careful. You don't understand how bad these men are."

He stared up at her, his eyes fierce with determination. "I won't let them hurt you, Mommy. I'll protect you."

She hugged him, fought back the tears. "Everything is going to be all right, Jamie. I swear."

She didn't know how, but she had to find a way to end this once and for all. But, God, she didn't have any idea where to begin. She couldn't depend upon the courts. She had no money for high-powered attorneys. Desmond would have the best…the absolute top in their fields. He would pay off the judge. He would win no matter what. And she would lose.

Fear shuddered through her. Just then, she did something she had never once in all these years done. She prayed that maybe Desmond was on his deathbed. As evil as he was, she had never wished him ill, only that he would leave her and her son alone. But today, as she held her unhappy child so close, she wished with all her heart that the bastard would die and go straight to hell where he belonged.

THAT NIGHT as Ashley helped clean up the kitchen after dinner, she watched her son play cards with Marla's daughters. At moments like this, he looked happy. He really did. Or was she fooling herself?

She paused, her hand stilling on the plate she was drying. "Is he like this most of the time?" Smiling, laughing, working hard to beat the girls at whatever game they were playing?

Marla leaned against the counter, her own work of putting away the dishes Ashley had dried momentarily on hold. "Yeah. Most of the time. Once in a while, I'll catch him acting a little down or distant. Not so often."

Ashley told herself that her friend's answer made her feel better, but did it? If her son was happy most of the time, did that mean he was getting used to his mother's absences? If she simply never came back, would he be better off? Be happier? An ache went through her making her breath catch. She couldn't do that.

"Ashley, listen to me." Marla took the plate and dish towel and set them aside. She took Ashley's hands in hers. "Your son loves you more than anything in this world. Not a day passes that he doesn't mention you."

She nodded. "I know. I guess I'm just feeling…" She shrugged. "I don't know…a little more desperate than usual, maybe."

Marla squeezed her hands. "Of course you are. You're watching your son grow up from a distance. It's hell on you."

"But I know he's in good hands," Ashley assured, not wanting to sound ungrateful. "It's just that I wonder how long we can keep this up."

"Trust yourself, Ashley. Trust your faith. God's looking out for you and your son."

Ashley hugged her dear, dear friend and then she did the hardest thing of all, she said goodbye to her son…again.

He took it like a champ. Far better than her, it seemed. She cried like a baby as she drove away, barely holding back the vicious onslaught of tears until she was out the door and out of his sight.

Replaying the moments she'd shared with her son that day only served to replenish the flood of emotions she couldn't quite control. They'd gone to his favorite park. Played hard. She'd acted like a kid herself. He'd selected lunch—hot dogs and sugary sodas and ice cream. Then they'd gone to the mall and he'd picked out a new model for his collection. He and the girls had checked it out before dinner.

She drove. Didn't let herself slow down for fear she'd turn around and rush back to spend the night as her son had begged her to do.

But she couldn't do that. Couldn't risk that her prolonged presence would put him in danger. As much as she loved and missed him, she couldn't take that chance.

He didn't understand.

He was only ten years old. How could he?

How did one make a child that young understand that his own father was pure evil? That merely being in his presence put them both at risk? Jamie didn't even know his father's name. As harsh as that sounded, she felt the step was necessary. If Jamie knew his father's name, he might grow curious and try to find out information about him. The Internet was a far too easily accessible tool for her to take that kind of chance.

So far, it hadn't been a problem. He hadn't asked. But her son was changing so fast it made her head spin. Each visit, she noticed more changes. What would she do when he demanded to know the whole truth?

Ice rushed through her veins and she strong-armed the subject to the back of her mind. She had enough problems right now without borrowing more.

Ashley swiped her eyes with the back of her hand, peered at the dark road ahead of her and considered again why, after all this time, Desmond would send someone looking for her and Jamie.

What did he want? Had new evidence on that old murder surfaced finally? Was he afraid she would go to the police when she heard?

She scanned all Chicago papers every day as a means of keeping up on anything Desmond might be up to. He'd kept a low profile the past three or four years. She imagined that he had plenty to keep him entertained without flaunting his wealth in the lime-light of society.

He'd always been a recluse. Preferring, as she'd learned too late, the dark, seamier side of society. Ashley thought back to her college days and tried to think what it was that had attracted her to him in the first place. He'd been so intriguing...so charming. Quiet and intelligent. She'd never met a man quite like him. Someone who could, at the snap of his fingers, fly to Paris for the weekend. Nothing was beyond his means. He had it all. Offered it all…or so it had seemed.

Then she'd learned the truth about her charming, distinguished, older man, who she had thought was her own personal knight in shining armor. He was addicted to every imaginable sexual perversion. He did a stellar job of keeping the ugly truth hidden. That was his reason for always having a young, beautiful woman like Ashley on his arm. From all appearances, he was a highly sought-after bachelor who had his pick of available women. No one bothered to look beyond that perfect picture.

Until it was too late.

Not that he'd let anyone. That was his reason for being so reclusive. The press couldn't report on what they didn't know.

She shuddered as she recalled the night she'd stumbled onto his collection of videos. It wasn't as if she'd been looking for trouble. She'd simply been bored.

The first few months they'd lived together, she had been Desmond's total focus. He'd spent every possible moment with her, had showered her with his attention and lavished her with gifts.

Then everything had changed, slowly at first, then blatantly. Most nights, he never even bothered to come home. There was always some business that kept him away. Especially after he'd learned she was pregnant. He'd scarcely touched her after that.

So she'd occupied herself in whatever ways she could find. Her boredom had sparked a need to explore one time too many and she'd found his secret room with its leather restraints and stark, steel cages.

Her questions had all been answered by the videos. Dozens upon dozens of documented recordings of his disgusting deviance.

She'd tried so hard to pretend she didn't know. To act as if nothing had changed. But he must have known somehow. The tension had been almost unbearable for months. Then their child had been born. Soon afterward, he'd persuaded her to return to his bed. A tremendous mistake. One night he'd lured her to that place where he played out his sick pleasures. She'd barely survived. The marks on her throat where he'd choked her had taken days to fade. He'd taunted her afterward telling her that if she ever told anyone she would only be setting herself up for ridicule since she was now one of his many filmed conquests. He knew people who could take his face out of the video and add anyone. The performance could end up on the Internet. And she could end up dead, he'd reminded her.

Knowing his secret perversion, staying with him had been tough enough when she had been pregnant.

She'd wanted to leave but her pregnancy had been a high-risk one. Extreme care had been required to ensure she carried the baby to term. Any attempts to escape him would have prompted physical and emotional stresses she couldn't have risked.

So she waited for just the right moment. And when Desmond least expected it, she'd run.

She hadn't stopped running since.

Ashley shook off the haunting memories and made the turn onto her street. She had to get her head back on straight if she intended to protect Jamie this time. No falling down on the job.

She glanced at her dash and noted that her gas tank was almost empty. Instead of driving to her little rented bungalow, she made the next right and headed back into town. She'd learned a long time ago never to go to bed at night with her gas tank nearly on empty. She never knew when she might have to make a run for it in the middle of the night. A full tank of gas stacked the deck a little more in her favor.

When she'd fueled up, she grabbed a bottle of water, paid the cashier and headed home.

It was past midnight. She had work tomorrow. She opened the bottle and took a long sip. Her throat was dry from too many tears and too much worry.

She was so tired of running.

As she turned back onto her quiet street, she wished again, that somehow, she could end this nightmare.

Chapter Four

It was past midnight.

Keith shook his head.

Where the hell was she? He'd been sitting here since nine that morning and nothing. He'd gotten out a couple of times and walked around the block to consider her small house from all sides. Since there was no vehicle in the drive and, according to Ben, she owned and presumably drove a black, twelve-year-old sedan, Keith doubted she was home.

He'd checked with a couple of her neighbors, pretending to be an insurance claims representative. The two he'd talked to knew basically nothing about Ashley, or Nola Childress as they called her. However, one did have information about where she worked since he shopped at the convenience store. Keith had gone by the store and she hadn't been there, either. He hadn't asked the clerk about Ashley's schedule to prevent the possibility of her being alerted to his presence.

He'd just about given up hope on her returning home that night when headlights bobbed at the far end of her street. He'd parked half a block from her house on the opposite side of the thoroughfare.

As the vehicle came nearer the size and color grew more visible. Black, four-door sedan.

His pulse quickened as the vehicle slowed and made the turn into the drive belonging to one Nola Childress, aka Ashley Orrick.

He watched her get out of the car. The hair was darker, an auburn maybe. According to Ben, the DMV showed her eyes to be brown, which was, of course, inaccurate. She wore jeans and a peach-colored blouse. She appeared alert to her surroundings as she moved up the sidewalk to her home. She unlocked the front door and went inside.

Lights glowed to life and he watched her silhouette cross in front of a couple of windows.

Keith opted not to carry his weapon, locking it in the glove box for safekeeping instead. The presence of a weapon would only add to the tension of the confrontation to come. He didn't consider her a threat physically so he saw no reason to go in armed.

As he was about to get out of his car, his cell phone vibrated and he fished it out of his pocket. "Devers."

"She just made a call to her mother."

Ben.

"Are they still talking?"

"Yeah. She's pretty much giving her a rundown on her day. She went to see her cousin and he's doing fine. Just so you know, she doesn't have a cousin."

Her son. She'd spent the day with her son. Keith's appearance at her mother's home had obviously spooked her. "They still talking?" He got out of his car and closed the door quietly behind him.

"Just hung up. She mentioned she didn't have to go back to work until the day after tomorrow."

Keith scanned the dark yards and houses on either side of his target's home. "Anything else?"

"Nope. I'll call you if there's anything new."

Keith ended the call and dropped the phone back into his pocket. He considered the conversation between Ashley and her mother. She was wrong. She wouldn't be going back to work the day after tomorrow. She had a command performance in Chicago and it was his job to make sure she showed.

Thankfully, no dogs started to bark as he walked the short distance to Ashley Orrick's small yard. He'd had a lot of time today to study her home. Though it was small, it was well kept. He imagined the recent exterior paint job was more about a good landlord than her desire to keep the place in shape. If her mother's home was any indication, any money the two were able to pool went to taking care of her son or was saved for financing her next escape in the event she was found rather than on household maintenance.

The car she drove indicated she didn't spend frivolously. There was nothing fancy about it. A definite budget model and well past its prime.

He wondered at that. As a younger woman, Ashley had moved into the home of a billionaire, had lived lavishly there for a year, during which time she produced his child. She abruptly disappeared and had since lived, seemingly, on the edge of poverty. It just didn't add up.

Of course it could be due to her alleged theft, but somehow that just didn't feel right. From what he'd learned about Ashley Orrick thus far, she was nobody's fool. Not by a long shot. The woman was very intelligent. There had to be a strong motivation for the decisions she'd made.

His curiosity had nagged at him since receiving this assignment. But it wasn't his job to understand why Ashley had taken the child, as well as the money, and run. His only concern was ensuring that Mr. Van Valkenberg had the opportunity to see his son.

The law provided for certain rights of the biological father. Ashley had to know that. Whatever her reasons for running, she had to come to terms with that undeniable truth. Van Valkenberg wanted nothing else from her.

Keith hoped convincing her of that fact wouldn't be too unpleasant for either of them. She seemed like a nice enough lady who perhaps was operating under some sort of misconceptions regarding the ex-boyfriend she'd lived with.

He slipped into the shadows at the side of her house away from the street light. She'd turned on the television; the sounds of a familiar network news channel filtered through the walls. A telephone rang. Didn't sound like a cell phone. Probably her land line. She answered. He listened for a minute or so more before he moved cautiously onto the narrow covered porch.

He waited until she'd hung up and then, cell phone in hand, he entered the land line number for Nola Childress. The phone inside the house rang again. Once, then twice.

"Hello."

Even through the protective walls of her rented home he could hear the trepidation in her voice. He pressed the End Call button as he simultaneously knocked on the front door.

When she didn't answer right away, he said loudly enough for her to hear his words clearly through the still closed door, "Ashley Orrick, I know you're in there. We need to talk. The matter is extremely urgent." For leverage, he tacked on, "I don't want to have to involve the police."

He braced himself for the shuffle of her running footsteps but the sound never came. Rather, the tumble of the lock being disengaged echoed and an overhead light pierced the darkness on the porch.

The door swung inward and determined brown eyes stared up at him. "Who are you?"

"I think you know who I am." No point in reciting information she already knew.

"I don't know how you found me, but your efforts have been wasted." She folded her arms over her chest and glared at him. "I know what you told my mother. I'm certain that isn't the whole story."

He gestured to the room beyond her position on the threshold. "May I come in? You don't have to worry, it's just me. No one's going to jump out of the bushes and try to ambush you while I have you distracted."

"I'm aware that you're alone." She stepped back for him to enter. "My neighbor just called and warned me that you'd been lurking around my neighborhood all day. He's probably watching right now. He won't forget your description or your license plate number, so this had better be legit."

He shrugged, not really surprised. It was a small community. Folks watched out for each other in close-knit neighborhoods. Not to mention a woman on the run would take precautions. But he'd had to try. "I guess I wasn't as convincing as I thought."

She didn't comment, just closed the door. As her hands fell to her sides, he noted that one fist was closed around a small bottle of pepper spray.

"What does he want?" she asked, keeping whatever she felt closely guarded.

At least she didn't beat around the bush when push came to shove. "Let's sit," he suggested hopefully, with a pointed glance at her weapon, "and talk about this calmly."

For a second or two she held her ground, then strode to the sofa and sat down. "Talk," she said as he chose the chair directly across from her.

"Mr. Van Valkenberg is not a well man," he said, getting right to the heart of the matter. He needed her cooperative, the best way to do that, he decided, was to give her some good news first. Since she obviously despised Van Valkenberg, his poor health would fall into that category. "He wants to know his son before—" he paused for emphasis and to weigh any reaction "—it's too late."

Like her mother, those assessing eyes narrowed suspiciously. "Are you telling me that he's dying?"

Keith had to work at not getting distracted by the sprinkle of freckles across her nose. The darker hair color only served to emphasize the trait that made her look far younger than her true age. He wondered how her eyes would look without the brown contacts. The vivid green in the old photographs he'd seen was a sharp contrast to this ordinary, everyday color she'd chosen as a part of her disguise. She must have gotten those from her father. Her mother's eyes had been gray.

Shifting his attention back to her question, he hedged somewhat in his answer, "He's very ill. That's all I'm at liberty to tell you at this time. He wishes to know his son and prepare him for his inheritance."

Her response to his explanation was the last thing he expected. She laughed. Long and loud.

He couldn't exactly call the sound unpleasant. Her laugh was rich and vibrant. It was the motivation behind the lapse in decorum that frustrated him, or maybe it surprised him. He hadn't taken her for such a coldhearted woman.

"You really expect me to believe that he cares about his son one way or the other? This is a new tactic, for sure."

Whatever she expected him to say to that, he could only answer with what he knew. "According to Mr. Van Valkenberg's representative, finding his son is his top priority. And his poor state of health is no laughing matter."

She rolled her eyes and pushed to her feet. "There is no way I'm telling you where my son is. So don't waste any more of your time. This meeting is over."

Keith stood, uncertain exactly what he'd said to rally this kind of reaction. Wasn't she interested in her son's financial future? "I'm not sure I understand the problem. We haven't discussed terms."

"There's nothing to discuss, Mr. Devers. You don't know Desmond Van Valkenberg. You've never even met him. Whatever his minion told you is a lie. I'm not letting him near my son. Now, I'd like you to go.

And don't bother relaying my address to your client. I'll be gone tomorrow."

A man couldn't ask for a woman to be any more straight forward than that. As frustrating as it was, he couldn't help admiring her strength.

"Then you leave me no choice." He reached into his interior jacket pocket for his cell phone. When she readied her can of spray, he showed her what was in his hand. "It's just a phone."

She relaxed marginally.

Not for long, he mused as he entered Ben's number. He might not be at the office but the guy wasn't married, so it wasn't as if Keith would wake up anyone else who might have gone to bed already. And he needed a second party to pull off this bluff.

When Ben answered, Keith said, "You'll need to awaken Mr. Brody and have him call me immediately. I need to give him an update on the situation." He ignored Ben's confused questions. "No, I'm afraid she refuses to cooperate." Keith hesitated. "Five minutes. Yes. I'll stand by."

When he closed the phone and dropped it back into his pocket, he allowed his full attention to return to the woman waiting two feet in front of him. All signs of cockiness had vanished. She looked seriously worried and just a little afraid.

"What're you doing?"

Now was the moment. He needed her to see that

there was no other choice. He needed that inkling of fear he saw in her eyes to morph into something that would prod her into cooperating.

"My orders are to bring you back to Chicago so that you and Mr. Van Valkenberg may discuss the issue of your son. If you refuse, I'm to provide your location and keep you under surveillance until he arrives."

Her posture stiffened slightly. "You're going to tell him where I am? He's coming here?"

"When Mr. Van Valkenberg's representative returns my call, I'm to give the location directly to him and no one else." He'd made that part up, but she didn't need to know.

"And if I run?" she asked, the wheels in her head turning frantically now. She realized her predicament. The ramifications played out in the genuine fear swiftly overtaking her expression.

"I'll follow you, keeping that representative abreast of your location every step of the way."

"My son isn't here," she challenged. "It won't do him any good to come here."

"But you're here," he countered. "And I'm certain you know where your son is. That's as far as my job goes. Apparently Mr. Van Valkenberg believes his people can handle the rest."

Her entire demeanor changed then. Keith wasn't exactly surely what part of his statement had made the difference but something had.

"I'm not giving you anything. I'll talk to Desmond face-to-face, but first I have to pack a bag."

The sudden about-face startled him.

When she turned to go to her room, he tagged along. "You won't mind if I keep you company."

It wasn't a question. She understood that.

He followed her to her room. After setting the can of pepper spray aside, she dragged a well used overnight bag from her closet and tossed a change of clothes inside. His cell phone rang and he told Ben the two of them were returning to Chicago shortly. For once, Ben was speechless. Maybe Keith's quick work surprised him.

Keith watched her wander about the room, gathering the usual items one would take on a trip away from home. He observed that she hadn't changed much, as the age progression results indicated. Still slender. Her hair hung down her back, shifted around her shoulders with her movements. Her hands shook once or twice, movements that tugged at his protective instincts. Long, delicate fingers and dainty wrists gave her a vulnerable appearance, but he sensed that she was a hell of a lot stronger than she looked. No matter how much strength she displayed, the situation made him feel a little like the bad guy.

She went into the bath directly across the hall, mumbling something about removing her contacts. He took a moment to covertly check her purse and to install a minor security measure before joining her. He loitered in the doorway of the modest-sized bathroom. Her gaze met his in the mirror and those vivid green eyes added another layer of uneasiness to his already growing discomfort.

"I guess I'm ready."

Her voice cracked a little, but she jutted her chin in defiance. Again, he had to admire her courage.

"Excellent."

She brushed past him on her way back into the bedroom and a feeling of regret washed over him. He shoved it away, had no intention of going there. She was the one who'd broken the law. More than one, if you counted depriving a father of his son. There was no place for sympathy here.

With her purse slung onto her shoulder, can of pepper spray inside, she reached for the overnight bag but he grabbed it first.

"My car is across the street and up the block a bit."

She nodded and led the way from the room. He took the same route, mentally kicked himself for noticing how nice her backside looked in those jeans. But then, he was only human.

With the lights out and the door locked they crossed the yard in silence. At the street, he said, "The gray sedan just over there."

She headed in that direction without comment. He dug for his keys and, using the remote, unlocked the doors. She slid into the passenger seat while he tossed her bag onto the backseat. He settled behind the wheel and started the engine.

ASHLEY REMAINED SILENT as he drove along her street away from the home she'd managed to hang on to for almost a year now. It wasn't that she would particularly miss the place, but she had enjoyed the stability for a change. Before Waynesville, her longest stint in a town had been six months.

Oh, well. Maybe that had been her mistake this time. She'd stayed put too long. Now she would pay the price.

She'd had just enough time after her neighbor called to stomp each of her three cell phones and hide them in the toilet tank. If they were ever found, she doubted if anyone could retrieve the numbers she had called. They had apparently already tracked her through her call to her mother. She could live with that. But she couldn't risk anyone getting their hands on Marla's number. That cell had actually been purchased in Marla's name, to prevent exactly what had most likely happened tonight.

She glanced at her hired escort. He had no idea whom he was dealing with. He obviously considered Mr. Van Valkenberg a nice man who'd been done wrong by his gold-digging ex-girlfriend. Ashley doubted there was much chance of changing this guy's opinion of her or his client. That left her only one option.

Escape.

She'd thought about spraying him back at her house and making a run for it. But that would have been a wasted effort. He had the make of her car and likely the license plate number. Tracking her down in her vehicle would be a cinch. Nope. She'd have to do something he wasn't expecting. Soon. She didn't want him to get her out of the state of Missouri. Thankfully, she had backup in place very close by.

There were some things she could rely on in Illinois but not so much as here. A feeling of bleakness settled over her. Maybe she'd put down deeper roots than she'd realized. She hadn't meant to.

Maybe she was just tired. Or older. Whatever the case, her relationship with Waynesville ended today. She could never come back.

The idea that her son resided in Springfield, less than two hours away, made her chest hurt. When would she be able to see him again? Even if she escaped today, she couldn't risk going to Jamie for at least several weeks. She would need new phones. Everything would have to change. Again.

That realization cut to the bone. She hated Desmond Van Valkenberg. She hoped he was dying. It couldn't be soon enough for her.

She told herself she should feel guilty for thinking

it, but she couldn't…wouldn't. He was a monster. No way was she going to let him get his hands on her son.

She would die first.

In the event she disappeared, Marla knew exactly what to do. She was to continue raising Jamie as if he were her own son.

Ashley blinked back the tears. She didn't want to think about the possibility of never seeing her son again. She loved him more than life. But she would deny herself the privilege of spending time with him if that was what it took to protect him.

"Have you eaten?"

Her attention shifted from the dark road ahead to the driver. Was he crazy? She was sitting here worried sick about her son and he wanted to know if she had eaten? Not to mention it was the middle of the night.

"Just drive, Mr. Devers." At least until he reached the exit she needed.

He didn't say anything else. She took a few moments to study him as he focused on driving. Why would Desmond send such a seemingly nice guy to bring her back? He usually dealt with thugs. This was a change of pace for him. Perhaps the concept of his mortality had softened him, though she seriously doubted that.

If by some stroke of bad luck she was unable to escape from this guy, that would be the one good thing about having to face Desmond again—laughing in his face if he truly was dying.

Ashley closed her eyes and leaned against the headrest. How had she gotten to this place? How could she relish the idea of a man's, any man's, imminent death? Hatred? Fear? She turned to the window and peered out into the darkness. Fear. She hated Desmond for what he'd done to her. She hated so many things about him, but she didn't wish him dead for his cruelty toward her. She wished him dead because she was scared of what he might do to her son.

How could she make people see that? Those who associated with Desmond on a professional level considered him above reproach. Just recently, she'd read about his generous donation to Chicago's Children's Hospital. How could anyone regard such a generous man any other way?

She turned her head just far enough to watch Keith Devers. He probably thought she was the worst kind of loser. A woman who'd used sex to gain entrance into a rich man's world. Then she'd disappeared, taking a major asset—the child—with her, depriving the father of his only son.

Oh, yeah. She was the villain. That would be Mr. Devers's opinion.

Whatever he thought of her, he was easy on the eyes. She almost laughed at herself for even allowing the thought. It had been so long since she'd looked at a man as anything but the enemy. It wasn't fair, she knew, but she just hadn't been able to trust any man since Desmond.

He'd damaged her heart too badly.

Devers sensed her watching him. He shoved a hand through his hair subconsciously. He had nice hair. Blond. Natural blond. Very tan. As Gina said, he had great blue eyes, too. Totally opposite from Desmond's dark features.

He tugged at his tie, again indicating his discomfort with her staring at him. His suit was a little rumpled. He'd hung out around her house all day, had probably driven all night the night before. He had to be exhausted. That would be to her benefit.

The upcoming exit number snagged her attention. This was the one.

"I need to use the bathroom."

He glanced at her, startled. "Now?"

"I can't hold it any longer. I've gotta go."

His brow furrowed. The light from the dash provided sufficient light for her to see his frustrated reaction. She bit her bottom lip to hold back a smile of triumph. Poor guy. He had no idea that he was about to make a huge mistake.

She'd done this too many times. Moved from town to town, always planning her backup strategy very carefully. He didn't stand a chance.

Not only did she lay out her escape routes with extreme caution, she also regularly checked each one. A girl never knew when a gas station or convenience store would shut down. She had to be smart, had to stay one step ahead of the enemy to survive. It helped that the owner of the convenience store where she worked owned several, one on each major route leaving Waynesville. And she knew them all.

"Stop there." She pointed to the upcoming all-night convenience store with its brightly lit neon sign and isolated islands of gas pumps. "This place'll be fine."

He parked in the lot. "I'll be right behind you," he warned as he opened his car door.

"Of course," she said. She hadn't expected otherwise. He wouldn't risk letting her get away.

Just as he promised, he followed her into the store, checked the ladies' room, and waited right next to the door while she went inside and did her business. It was almost too easy.

She wondered how long he would wait before coming inside to find out what was keeping her.

Then again, it really didn't matter because she'd be long gone.

Chapter Five

From his position propped against the wall next to the ladies' room door, Keith watched the customers go about their business inside the gas station's convenience store. Most came in for cigarettes and beer, as well to pay for their gas.

Thankfully, no one paid any particular attention to him. He considered fueling up since they'd stopped. He could do that when he had Ashley Orrick safely tucked back into the car. No way would he risk letting her out of his sight. Beyond the ladies' room, anyway.

He glanced at his watch. Three minutes. She'd been in there long enough to relieve herself. Her cell phone hadn't been in her purse, so she couldn't be attempting to make a call. Still, he didn't like giving her this much time outside his line of vision.

He gave a quick rap on the door. "What's taking so long in there?" He waited for a response. Ten seconds later, the answering silence sent his pulse into triple time.

He twisted the knob and pushed against the door. Locked. Swearing under his breath, he strode over to the counter, keeping one eye on the door. "I'm going to need a key to the ladies' room." Kicking in the door would only prompt the attendant to call the police and he didn't need that kind of trouble.

The man behind the counter stared at him with a "yeah, right" expression. The clerk shook his head. "Don't waste your time, buddy. If she ain't answering the door, she probably climbed out the window."

Keith frowned. "What window? I looked in there before she went in. There was no window."

His shiny bald head hitched in the direction of the locked door. "You saw the utility rack holding the toilet paper and paper towels?"

Keith nodded. "Against the far wall next to the sink."

The clerk smirked. "We put it there to hide the window. Keeps 'em from taking merchandise in the bathroom and going out the window with it. The owner keeps saying he's gonna close it up, but he don't. I guess your friend's been here before."

Keith was out the door before the man finished his last smug statement. Sure enough, at the back of the building, a window leading into the ladies' room had been opened.

Swearing at himself for falling for her trick, he

yanked out his handheld computer and logged onto the tracking software Ben had downloaded for him. A map of the area flickered onto the screen and then a blinking red cursor monitored his target's movements.

As long as she didn't ditch her purse, he was good to go. Looked like that security measure he'd put into place had paid off after all.

When he'd rounded up the flashlight from the trunk of his car and his weapon from the glove box, he headed into the woods behind the station. He didn't worry about her point of entry. He had the co-ordinates of her current location, all he had to do was close in on that mark. And not break his neck stumbling through the woods in the damned dark.

He mentally kicked himself a few more times. She had to know this area damn well to attempt this route in the dark. He should have realized when she surrendered so easily that she was up to something. Instead, he'd foolishly hoped that somehow during the long drive back to Chicago he could talk her into divulging the whereabouts of her son and saving everyone a lot of trouble.

Fat chance.

He paused long enough to determine where she might be headed if she continued on her current course and his best estimate was a small community called St. Robert's between Waynesville and the military base Ft. Leonard Wood. A ten- to twelve-mile trek through dense forest, the first four or five miles at a steadily inclining grade.

She moved far faster than him, another indication that she knew the route. She had to be on a trail of some sort. Maybe an old hunting route. He was certain she didn't have a flashlight, unless she'd had one of those hidden in that convenience store bathroom, too.

His best bet would be to take a few minutes and attempt to find the trail in hopes of facilitating his advancement. Otherwise—he swore when a branch he released too soon smacked him in the face—he was going to have to fight nature the entire route.

Ten minutes later he discovered the narrow path that cut through the ever-thickening underbrush. She'd gained a sizable advantage over him by then, but he would recover the lost ground. He broke into a steady jog. He couldn't risk a dead run, considering the trail took unexpected turns and dips and tree limbs and bushes extended across the trail in places.

Each time a tree limb slapped him, he thought of a new way to make his target pay.

All he had to do was catch her.

ASHLEY STOPPED to catch her breath. It would be daylight soon. She was almost there…maybe another hundred yards. The zigzagging route she'd taken had kept her well ahead of her pursuer. But she knew he was out there. She could feel him coming.

She leaned against the trunk of a tree and closed her eyes. She thought of her son and how disappointed he would be when she couldn't come to see him this weekend. Her only promise had been that she would try, but he would cling to that as if she'd given a solemn vow.

God, she hated Desmond for doing this to them.

Her eyes popped open and she stilled, listened intently. Devers had almost caught up with her once. She'd been surprised that, wearing a suit of all things, he could track her so well in the dark and across unfamiliar terrain.

And then she'd realized. He'd probably put some sort of device in her purse. She might not be a cop or federal agent, but she'd watched enough television and movies to understand the technology they used.

So she'd taken one necessary item from her purse and she'd tossed the bag into a ravine. That bag, like every other thing in her life—except her son, of course—was expendable.

Her muscles relaxed when no other sound vibrated against her senses. She had to smile. She could just see him schlepping down that slope to see if she'd fallen to her death.

Okay, so that wasn't exactly funny. She didn't wish Mr. Devers any ill will or physical injury, but he was, in reality, the enemy.

Outwitting him was essential, even if it did involve a scratch or two to his handsome mug.

She got to her feet and dusted off her backside. No point in waiting around to see if he would catch up with her again. She wanted to be long gone by the time he stumbled into the clearing just up ahead.

Clutching the key to her escape in her hand, she headed for the tree line. As she neared the edge of the woods a hum or vibration of some sort had her listening as hard as she could. A motor?

She reached the treeline and surveyed the old hunting shack before venturing from the safety of her cover. Imagine her surprise when she noted lights on in the shack. She hadn't even known there was electricity this far back in the boonies.

There wasn't, she realized. The hum she heard was a generator.

Damn.

How was she supposed to get her car with trespassers hanging out in that shack?

Well, she supposed the people could own the place. But she'd been told the shack was abandoned, had been for two decades. The land owners had donated the whole kit and caboodle to the Army base. There wasn't supposed to be anyone out here. So whoever was in there couldn't be the owners.

Unless it was some sort of military exercise.

That wouldn't be good.

Wasn't trespassing on military property some sort of federal offense?

She eased around the perimeter of the clearing to take a look at any vehicles that might be parked on the other side of the shack.

To call the spot a clearing wasn't exactly accurate. The overhead canopy of older, larger trees was still thick high overhead, but the smaller ones had been cut away years ago in an area of about half an acre. Lots of bushes and saplings had sprouted up over the years making the place look overgrown. A dilapidated shack stood smack in the middle and what passed for a road meandered off into the woods. It came out along a country road in the middle of nowhere, but it was rough going any way but by foot. It hadn't been used by vehicles in years, except for her occasional visit.

Until now, that is.

Her mouth dropped open when she saw that her old Jeep had been moved. She'd purchased it and parked it here months ago. Each time she drove it around, she parked back in the same spot. The trespassers had obviously hot-wired it and used it for their own purposes. Which meant she had no way of knowing how much gas might be in the tank. Next to the Jeep was an equally run-down truck. What looked like garbage had been piled against the side of the shack. Another pile, partially covered by a blue tarp sat nearby.

Definitely not military.

How long had these people been here?

She bit back a stinging curse. How was she supposed to get out of here now?

Calm down. Three deep breaths. She might still be able to do this. It wasn't daylight yet. If she could get to the Jeep and get it started before anyone came outside…

But what if the battery was dead? She came by routinely to check on it. Even started it up and drove it around the clearing a couple of times every month or so. But knowing her luck, the battery would be dead, or the gas tank would be empty, and she'd be screwed. She hadn't been here in two or three weeks. A lot could have happened in that length of time.

Obviously.

She eased down onto her haunches and fought the urge to admit defeat and just keep walking toward her destination. She might make it by noon, assuming Devers didn't catch up with her. She'd formed contingency plans for everything. There were a dozen ways in and out of here, each ending up at a different destination. She knew every single one by heart. But, damn, she could use that Jeep.

Her neighbors watched her house when she was at work. Her coworkers and boss kept an eye on any strangers who hung around the store. She was so thorough.

This escape route had been her ace in the hole.

She'd figured that whoever came after her, if she was located, would be armed or, at the very least, bigger than her. She couldn't have hoped to fight them off physically. Killing another human was out of the question—though she had no problem wishing death on the monster who held such a threat over her head. Her only alternative had been to plan carefully. No man ever wants a woman to "go" in his car. No matter how tough, he'll stop at the nearest bathroom. Stopping along the highway and forcing her to "go" in the open would run the risk of being noticed by a cop or passerby.

She'd had it all figured out.

And it had worked.

Up to the part where she got away clean.

That old Jeep had been her ticket out of here.

A man staggered out the back door of the shack. Dawn had brightened the early morning hour to the point that she could vaguely make out his features.

Fortyish. Grungy jeans and T-shirt.

When he peeled open his fly she turned her head in the nick of time.

So maybe attempting to get the Jeep wasn't such a good idea. Walking to her destination wouldn't be the worst thing she'd ever had to do. As long as she didn't let Devers catch up with her.

The grungy guy staggered back into the shack, slammed the wooden door. The thwack echoed in the clearing, made her shiver. Or maybe it was the early morning mist that had settled on her skin. When it was this damp at daylight, mega humidity could be expected as the temperature rose.

Perfect for walking, she mused.

She could make her way along the tree line to the other side of the clearing and pick up the trail that would take her back to some semblance of civilization. The idea of hitchhiking wasn't very appealing, but a lot of military folks traveled those roads. She might feel comfortable accepting a ride from someone in uniform.

Desperate times called for desperate measures.

Right now, she was about as desperate as a woman could get and still be breathing on her own.

Her nose twitched. What was that smell?

Something chemical…something foul.

Evidently she'd been too caught up in worry about the Jeep to notice the smell.

Careful to remain hunkered down out of sight, she edged back a little farther into the concealing depths of the forest. Maybe she didn't want to know who these people were or why they had spoiled her contingency plan after all. She had a bad feeling they were up to something extremely dangerous and seriously illegal.

A hand abruptly wrapped around her mouth and jerked her body backward into what felt like a brick wall.

"Don't even think about making a noise," a masculine voice growled against her ear.

Devers.

Fury chased away the fear and before she could stop the impulse she elbowed him hard in the ribs.

He grunted but didn't let go.

"You scream and we'll both be in trouble," he warned. Slowly he loosened his grip on her mouth.

She wheeled around and glared at him through the minimal light filtering down from the canopy of trees. "You scared the hell out of me," she snapped in a stage whisper.

"Yeah, well, you'll get over it," he grumbled under his breath. "I can't say the same for these shoes."

She looked him up and down the best she could with him crouched only a couple feet in front of her. His tie hung loosely around his throat. His shirt had enough wrinkles to give it that crinkled look and looked a lot less white than before. The suit, with a torn sleeve and pocket, appeared beyond salvaging. But the shoes had hands down taken the worst damage. She imagined that the descent and then the upward climb out of that ravine had finished them off. No amount of polish would ever make them look shiny and new again. Too bad.

"Do you always stalk your prey in Armani?" She couldn't keep the amusement out of her tone. He was just too handsome for his own good and clearly he prided himself on an elegant appearance. Between the tousled hair and the battered clothes, he might even be considered adorable…if he weren't the enemy. It was impossible not to notice.

Where the hell had Desmond found this guy? He was not the usual sort her ex associated with.

"There is nothing even remotely amusing about this situation, Miss Orrick," he growled quietly. "In case you haven't noticed, the people in that shack are preparing illegal drugs."

Ashley's heart lunged into her throat. Not because of anything he said but because of the business end of the shotgun that came into view behind him.

Apparently her look of horror alerted Devers to the situation and he whipped around to face the man, lunging to a standing position with amazing agility.

Men, she amended, as she stood a little slower and peeked around Devers's broad shoulder. Three altogether. All sporting the same grungy look as the fellow she'd first seen emerge from the shack this morning.

"Let's see some ID, pretty boy," the one with the gun aimed at Devers's chest ordered.

"Looks like a Fed to me," one of the others said, his own weapon aimed at Devers as well.

The third man appeared intent on analyzing Ashley. She moved in closer behind Devers. She didn't really know him, but he was a fair-sized guy and not once had he made her feel as if her honor might be in jeopardy. She doubted he could take all three of these guys, but he might provide enough of a distraction to give her the opportunity to run like hell.

But that would only get him killed.

Any hope of escaping this mess withered.

They were in big trouble.

Devers reached into his jacket for his ID and the guy who'd been eyeing Ashley bolted into action, slamming the butt of his shotgun into the side of Devers's head with such force that he hit the ground like a rock without the slightest reaction or attempt to catch himself.

Ashley dropped to her knees. Cringed at the blood that bloomed and then oozed down the side of his face. Not good. She surveyed his chest. At least he was still breathing.

"Bring her to the kitchen," the one apparently in charge commanded.

She tried to scramble away but she wasn't fast enough. Steel fingers manacled her arm.

"Bring him, too," the boss called over his shoulder as he stalked away. "We got to figure out what to do with their bodies."

Ashley's heart slammed mercilessly against her ribcage. She had never fainted in her life but just now she felt dangerously close to doing just that.

The man ogling her ushered her into the clearing. She looked back once, just long enough to see the other guy dragging Devers by the collar of his elegant jacket.

Oddly, the one thought that crossed her mind was that now his trousers would be ruined, too.

PAIN SHATTERED his skull.

Keith groaned.

He struggled to open his eyes but somehow his brain wouldn't issue the proper command.

Something was wrong. There were things he needed to do. Important things but he couldn't make himself wake up long enough to do anything about it.

He held his breath as another jolt of pain knifed through him.

What the hell was wrong with him?

His body shook hard. Why couldn't he stop shaking?

He could hear a voice. The sound was far away. Unfamiliar.

The shaking started again. Harder this time. He tried to control it, but couldn't.

"Devers, wake up!"

He understood his name. Someone kept telling him to wake up. Over and over the voice told him. But he couldn't make it happen.

"Devers, you have to wake up. Open your eyes!"

Something or someone prodded one eyelid open. He blinked. Shook his head. The pain radiated outward from the center of his skull like shards of glass exploding in his brain.

"Open your eyes, dammit. We have to get out of here!"

With monumental effort, he managed to open his eyes just a crack. Enough to see that he was in a dark place. It smelled musty and dank.

A piercing light shined into his eyes.

He jerked away from it, howled with pain from abrupt movement.

"Thank God," the voice said. "I thought you were dead for a minute there."

Time and place crashed down around him.

Waynesville, Missouri.

Ashley Orrick.

Meth lab.

He forced his eyes open again. The light was still on but not aimed at his face.

"I found this in your jacket pocket. It's a miracle it didn't fall out while that guy was dragging you across the clearing."

Dragging?

Oh, yeah, he remembered. That was why his head was throbbing and felt like a damaged melon. The guy had popped him with the butt of his rifle.

Jerk.

He quickly felt for his weapon.

"They took everything else. Your gun. Cell phone. Wallet. I don't know why they didn't take the light. Maybe they didn't notice it."

"Are you all right?" His voice sounded rusty and the effort it took to talk added another layer of discomfort to the mix of unpleasant sensations assaulting him.

She nodded. "I thought for a while I might have some trouble out of one of the guys, but apparently we caught them at a bad time."

Keith eased up just enough to lean back on what he decided was another part of the ground that made up the walls of their prison. A cave? he wondered vaguely. "How's that?" The place smelled exactly like a cave.

"They had to get their latest batch of meth delivered. At least that's what I think they were talking about. They didn't want to wait. I heard one of them tell the others that they would take care of us when they got back. That's why I've been trying to wake you up. We have to get out of here before they get back."

Keith examined his forehead and right temple gingerly. "How long have they been gone?"

"An hour, maybe."

He looked around. "Where are we?"

"An old root cellar under the shack. They locked us in. I tried busting the lock, but I couldn't do it. Outside of digging our way out, I figure that's our only means of escape. Digging could very well take forever."

He touched his left wrist but his watch was gone.

"They took that, too."

"How long have I been unconscious?"

She shrugged. "An hour and a half, maybe. I can't be sure. Could be two hours."

Okay. He had to think. She was right. They might not have much time.

They were inside the shack. Under the floor of the run-down structure. No way to get out from underneath without, as she said, digging. Even if they had shovels that would take too long. The door was locked.

An idea occurred to him. "Have you ever been in this old shack before?"

"No. I mean, I've been here but never inside."

"Well." He scrambled to his feet, staggered. She steadied him.

"Thanks," he mumbled as he reached up and pressed against the floorboards overhead. "If the interior is as dilapidated as the exterior, the lock on that door may be the strongest part of our prison. Are there any steps leading up?"

"This way." She tugged him across the small root cellar.

Four steps had been carved out of the earth and led up to a trapdoor in the floor.

"Okay, let's push next to the door, away from the lock."

"I follow," she said. "The floor could be easier to bust through if the wood is as dry rotted as the rest of the place. My mistake was focusing on the lock."

"Exactly." He pushed on a couple of loose boards. It would take some work, but it was possible.

"I should have thought of this." As she said each word she shoved hard against first one floor board, then another.

Using all his strength, which wasn't saying much, Keith forced his body weight against the flooring overhead. Ashley mimicked his moves.

"This one's coming loose!"

He moved closer to her and together they shoved enough boards loose from the deteriorating cross beams to get her through the opening.

She pried up another board and reached her hand through to assist him in climbing out.

Their gazes collided and for one instant he was stunned by the idea that she would help him when he was, for all intents and purposes, her enemy.

"Come on," she urged. "We don't have all day."

He took her hand and maybe it was his imagination, or the concussion he likely had just received, but something electrical flashed over his skin, made him shiver.

Shock. He was likely suffering from some degree of shock. That explained it.

With Ashley's help, he struggled out of the dark prison. The overwhelming chemical odor hanging in the air aboveground made him cough.

"Stinks, huh?" She assisted him to his feet.

"Yeah." He surveyed the room. Didn't see any sign of his cell phone, pocket PC or weapon.

"We gotta go," she urged.

He nodded. Wished he hadn't when pain splintered in his head. He staggered again. She steadied him once more.

"Maybe you'd better lean on me."

She led him out into the daylight and into the cover of the trees. They'd gotten no more than twenty yards into the forest when he heard the distant sound of engines.

"They're back." She peered toward the shack. "As soon as they realize we've escaped, they'll be looking for us."

Keith pulled away from her. "You're right. That's precisely what they'll do. I can't run. I can barely walk." He exhaled a shaky breath. "You go. Send someone back for me."

"For you?" she asked archly. "Don't you mean for your body?"

"Just go, Ashley."

She looked startled that he used her first name.

"There's no reason for both of us to die," he pointed out.

"That's right." She grabbed his arm. "I know a place we can hide until dark. Then we'll get out of here. They can't possibly know these woods better than me. With the cover of darkness on my side, I can lose them."

Still he hesitated. "You sure about this?"

"Stop stalling, Devers." She tugged him forward. "We don't have time for deliberation."

He let her lead him.

It didn't really matter where so he didn't ask questions.

She was the only chance they had of surviving this day.

Chapter Six

She had to be out of her mind.

Ashley stared at the sleeping man. She should just leave him. This was her chance.

Wringing her hands, she crouched behind the bushes that provided their only cover in the little bluff alcove nature had burrowed into the rocks. The bad guys had already passed twice, once in the heat of the chase looking for their prey, the last time some two hours later as they trudged back to the shack empty-handed. She'd heard them arguing and cursing. They were more than a little angry that the man and woman had gotten away. One had grumbled that, under the circumstances, moving their kitchen couldn't be put off.

Ashley shuddered at the thought of the dangerous drugs these lowlifes cooked up.

She was glad they were going. She'd felt as if that shack was hers for a year now.

Not that their departure would do her any good. The drug cookers weren't the only ones who would have to change venue.

She glanced back at Keith Devers.

She would have to move, as well.

Staying in Waynesville was out of the question now. Maybe she could get lost in St. Louis. She hated to move too far away from Jamie.

No matter, she definitely had to go. Worry gnawed at her. To be honest, remaining in this state might not even be a good idea.

If she had any sense, she'd be long gone right now. Her gaze shifted back to the man who'd propelled her into this mess. She'd gotten him away from the immediate danger of those scumbags. If she left him now, he'd probably be fine. *If he doesn't stumble right back into those nasty guys,* a little voice warned.

She sighed wearily. Why did she care? It would be dark in a few hours and she needed to get as far away from here as possible.

She had her own best interest to consider.

Since she didn't have a watch or cell phone and neither did her companion, she couldn't say exactly what time it was. Noon had come and gone, she recognized by the position of the sun. It could be three o'clock, could be four. She was starving and thirsty, but she was alive.

She crept back over to Devers and studied him.

He'd groaned a couple of times in the last hour. He'd awakened and sat propped against the rocks off and on all morning, but then he'd slept most of the afternoon, which worried her a little. She'd woken him at frequent intervals just to make sure he was still alive. That wasn't really true. If he had a concussion, as she suspected, or even a contusion, waking him frequently was the recommended course of action. She vaguely remembered that from some safety course she'd taken ages ago.

Poor guy. His swollen cheek and the lump near his temple looked seriously painful. He hadn't mentioned it, but she was certain he'd had a major headache when he came to that first time. She imagined that was why he sat so still and quiet. Movement or speech would have added to his suffering.

He had nice hair. Thick, blond. And Gina was right: he did kind of look like one of those surfer guys with the kind of tan one nurtured on a sandy beach. Blue eyes like the water that would roll across that same sand.

The route her thoughts had taken surprised her. She hadn't lusted after a guy in a really long time. That the object of her admiration was her current enemy only made matters worse.

She really needed to get her sex life in order when she settled in her next location. It just wasn't normal for a woman to go without the attention of a man for so long.

Then again, it was a man's attention that had started this whole nightmare.

That was just wrong. She chastised herself for thinking such a thing. If she hadn't met Desmond, she wouldn't have Jamie.

Jamie. She plopped onto her bottom near her patient. She'd named her son Avery when he was born. Running away had required a change in more than scenery. She had become Nola and he'd become Jamie. He wasn't even aware he'd ever had any other name.

All the lies and the deception, that was the saddest part of all. Her son's entire life was based upon a pyramid of untruths. She couldn't help wondering if he would hold that against her one day.

Her gaze rested on Devers again. And if what he said about Desmond's health was true, their freedom might very well be close at hand. It wasn't right that she let herself feel that way. Desmond was human, after all. She shouldn't wish for his demise.

But she did.

She hated him for what he'd done to her and their child. He cared about no one but himself. She could not bring herself to believe that he would ever, in a million years, care about his son. This whole child support and estate thing was likely nothing more than an elaborate trick to lure her into a trap.

She had to get out of here. Warn her mother and then disappear.

A weariness she'd never felt before settled over her. She was tired. Tired of running. No matter how many times she'd done it before, this time felt different. Maybe she was different.

Whatever the case, she had no other option. Staying was out of the question.

All she had to do was figure out what she would do with him.

A dog howled in the direction of the shack.

A new kind of fear shivered up her spine.

More howling. At least two dogs.

She shook Devers. He groaned. "Wake up, Devers," she urged.

He struggled up onto his elbows and forced his eyes open. "What's wrong?"

"Dogs." As if to punctuate the one word howling echoed through the trees. "They've got dogs now."

"Water."

She frowned. "What?" She was thirsty, too, but this was no time to think about a drink.

"We need water." Swaying a little, he managed to achieve a respectable sitting position. "They can't pick up our scent in water."

"Oh, I get it. Like walking through a stream."

"That would do it." He scrubbed his hair back, careful of his injury. "You know where there's a handy stream around here?"

She laughed giddily, panic nipping at her heels. "As a matter of fact I do."

After helping Devers to his feet, she held on to his hand and moved as quickly as she felt she could with him in tow. Maybe she was just lucky, or maybe God was looking out for them, but the stream they needed wasn't far from their current location.

When she'd found it the first time, she remembered thinking how it might come in handy some time. She'd gone back to it each time she came this way just to make sure she recalled the route to take. The stream meandered through the woods for about a mile then spilled into a narrow snaking river.

She just hoped that the long hot July days hadn't dried the stream to a trickle.

Maybe their luck would hold out.

KEITH LEANED against a tree to catch his breath.

Damn, he hadn't felt this weak in…he couldn't remember ever feeling this useless. He could walk, but running was out of the question. His head didn't ache quite so bad as a few hours ago. And the dizziness had eased up a bit. The nausea, well, that was a different story.

He closed his eyes and fought back a wave of nausea. Apparently the guy had been trying to kill him versus knocking him unconscious.

When his gut had calmed, he opened his eyes

once more and watched the woman survey the road beyond the tree line. It wasn't quite dark yet, but wading through that stream and then crossing the river had given them an edge on their pursuers.

According to his reluctant guide, they had arrived at a highway she knew well. She was now watching for a car that she might wave down for a ride.

The one thing he couldn't do was let her get out of his sight. In his current condition, he didn't want to find himself trying to run her down.

Bracing for the pain, he pushed off the tree and took the half-dozen or so steps that separated them. His shoes were still soggy but his trouser legs were pretty much dry.

"Anything yet?"

She didn't look at him, just shook her head. "Don't worry, though. Someone will come along."

He wondered if her frequent upheavals had enabled her to maintain such an optimistic attitude in the face of dour conditions. To date, he hadn't seen anything get her down. Not even a handful of drug thugs.

"Here we go." She nodded toward the headlights in the distance.

"Wait long enough to be sure it's not a pickup truck," he suggested, not wanting to run into the thugs again. He was unarmed and pretty much helpless.

"It's a car," she said after a moment's consideration.

When she was about to step clear of the trees, he grabbed her by the arm and held her back. "Maybe I should stick with you."

She rolled her eyes. "I won't leave you, Devers."

He tried to read her eyes only she wasn't allowing that. But he had to confess, she hadn't left him yet and she'd had ample opportunity. "All right."

Ashley Orrick slipped out of the woods and rushed toward the pavement, waving madly.

All he needed was a phone. One call to Ben and he'd have everything he needed within a few hours. First he had to get to civilization.

Incredibly, the car stopped. Keith refrained from the urge to shake his head. He couldn't believe people still did that. A hitchhiker could turn out to be a serial killer. As could the kind of driver who would pick up a hitchhiker, he countered. The thought had him easing farther into the open.

The driver apparently agreed to her request. Ashley looked back toward his location. As Keith was about to step out of the woods, she wrenched the front passenger door open and jumped in. The car roared off.

It took three seconds for his brain to catch up with his eyes.

He lunged out of the woods. Scrambled down and then up the ditch that separated the forest from the pavement. But he was too late to get the license plate number.

Fury burned through him. More at his own stupidity than at her resourcefulness.

He should have expected her to run. She'd gotten him out of danger and now she had to protect herself.

"Dammit!"

He started walking.

What choice did he have?

What was the likelihood that anyone would pick him up? He looked a mess, his head was bleeding.

Nada.

He hadn't gotten far when he heard the sound of a car coming. It was going in the opposite direction from the one Ashley had taken, but, hey, beggars couldn't be choosers. Right now he just needed a lift.

And a phone.

As the vehicle neared, astonishment washed over him, making him dizzy. This time, it had nothing to do with his head injury.

It was the same car Ashley had hopped into and taken off in.

The car stopped in front of him and Ashley leaned toward the driver and shouted past him. "Sorry, I guess I forgot about you."

The driver looked skeptical but didn't say anything.

She hitched her thumb toward the backseat. "Hop in. Larry's going to give us a ride into town."

Keith didn't question her change of heart, he climbed into the back seat and Larry took off.

He watched Ashley as she chatted with their Good Samaritan about how their car had broken down so many miles back that she couldn't even remember how long they'd been walking. Larry grunted a couple of times but didn't say much. He seemed too enthralled with the lady's voice.

Keith had to admit that the sound was very pleasant. Pretty lady, sweet voice.

What was the deal with her?

She'd been running for ten years. Had painstakingly kept her son hidden from his father. Why hadn't she run when she had the chance? Chances, actually. She'd had several.

Hell, he'd been unconscious for most of the afternoon. It wasn't as if she'd left him with those thugs. She'd gotten him to safety when he damned sure hadn't been able to help himself.

He didn't get it.

Exhaustion kept him from pondering the question any longer. Whatever the answer, he was glad she hadn't run out on him.

As grateful as he was, her act of compassion changed absolutely nothing.

He had a job to do, and he intended to do it as long as he was still breathing.

By the time they reached Waynesville, it was dark.

Ashley thanked the driver profusely. Keith let her do the talking. She hadn't stopped since the guy had picked them up. He couldn't figure out if she was nervous or just trying to make the guy feel comfortable with two haggard strangers in his car.

"I need a shower," she said as she reached under a rock near the steps for her hidden spare key. "But first I have to have some food and water." She climbed the steps and crossed the porch.

Keith looked down at himself. He could use a shower as well, but finding clothes, well that would have to wait until he'd reached Ben.

Inside, she led the way to the kitchen, flipping on lights as she went. "Will your friends come looking for you since you didn't report in today?"

He leaned against the doorjamb. He'd been doing a lot of leaning today. "Why do you ask?"

She grabbed a couple of bottles of water from the fridge and handed one to him. "I'm just trying to decide if I made a mistake when I had Larry go back to pick you up."

Keith twisted the cap off his water and downed half of it before he stopped. It felt good sliding down his parched throat. Man, he hadn't realized just how thirsty he was.

When he wiped his mouth with his hand, he asked, "Why did you come back?"

She'd finished off most of her water, as well. "I don't know." Her shoulders lifted, then fell. "Felt like the right thing to do." She downed the last of her water. "Go ahead and find something to eat. I've gotta get in that shower."

When she reached the door, he said, "Thanks for saving my ass back there."

She looked back at him for several moments before she responded. "No problem. Just don't make me regret it."

Funny thing was, he already regretted what he knew he had to do.

ASHLEY STOOD under the hot spray of water and relished the sensation of warmth. It felt good gliding down her skin, washing away the day's stress and grime.

She closed her eyes and washed her hair, letting her fingers knead her scalp a little while longer than necessary. She was so tired. But did she dare sleep?

Her top priority had to be giving Devers the slip. There was no reason to worry about him now. There was food, water and a phone here. He wouldn't need any further assistance from her.

As the shampoo suds slid down her skin she mentally kicked herself for being a total idiot. She should have left him on the side of the road. He would have been fine. Someone else would have come along and even if they hadn't stopped, they would probably have called the police to report an injured man wandering along the road.

No. She'd had to play the hero. Doing the whole

neighborly thing. Now she'd lost her edge. And most assuredly her head start on whatever Desmond was up to.

She scrubbed at her hair, rinsing it clean. A dozen times in the past ten years, she'd picked up in the middle of a perfectly good life and walked away without looking back.

Why in the world had she looked back today?

And that was what she'd done. She'd stared out that rear window and saw him standing by the side of the road all alone and she hadn't been able to put the image out of her head.

She'd ended up talking Larry into going back for him. She'd covered herself by telling him that she and Devers had had a fight and she'd planned to just leave him there to show him who was boss. But she hadn't been able to follow through with it. Dear old Larry had fallen for her story all the way to her insistence that she and Devers would live happily ever after.

Yeah, right. Hadn't she learned the hard way that there were no happily ever afters? No knights in shining armor. Fairy tales were just that…tales…fiction.

She couldn't totally explain today's lapse in judgment but she was back on track now. The first chance she got, she was out of here. Too much was at stake for her to behave this stupidly for no good reason.

In a hurry now, she quickly cleansed her body,

then stepped out onto the fuzzy bathmat. She wrapped a towel around her hair and her body and headed to her room for fresh clothes.

In the hall outside the bathroom, she drew up short.

Keith Devers waited there for her.

"I had a sandwich. Made one for you, too."

She blinked, tried to decide what to say, but it was difficult with him looking at her that way. His cheeks flamed ever so slightly and he turned away about the same time that she realized that she was standing there in nothing but a skimpy towel.

"A sandwich? Great. I'll just get some clothes first."

Could she sound any more lame?

She dashed to her bedroom and slipped on clean undies, jeans and a T-shirt. Before going out of her room, she quickly prepared a getaway bag with sneakers, socks, another change of clothes and one of the five toiletry kits she kept ready for takeoff. She hid the bag between her bed and the wall.

With her hair still in a towel, she left her room. Found Devers waiting for her in the hall.

"Don't you want a shower?" He had to be feeling sticky and dirty all over just as she had.

"Yeah, that'd be great, but there's a little problem."

She tensed. "What kind of problem?"

He flared his hands as if he hated to bring up the subject. "I'm still having a problem with dizziness. I'm not sure I can trust myself in a slippery shower."

Suspicion reared its ugly head. "What do you want me to do?" She should never have asked the question.

"If you could just make yourself handy. You know, be in the room while I shower. I'll be quick," he added hopefully.

What could she say? She'd asked for it.

With her back to the shower, she stood in the bathroom, her arms crossed over her chest. She was out of her mind. That was the only possible explanation.

If listening to him shed his clothes hadn't been bad enough, now she had to hear him moan at the feel of the hot water sluicing over his skin. Of course she understood that it felt great after what they'd been through. His muscles were likely aching. His head probably still hurt. The heat from the water would relax him and make him feel immensely better.

The runaway thoughts had images forming in her head that she didn't need to see, now or ever.

All the splashing, moaning and sighs of relief were just about more than she could take. Clearly there was no reason for her to be in the room. He had everything under control.

"Could you hand me that towel?"

The deep sound of his voice raked over her already raw nerves and she jumped.

"Sorry. I didn't mean to startle you. But I forgot my towel."

She grabbed the towel from the stool and handed

it back to him, careful to keep her eyes directly in front of her. Turning around was out of the question.

Closing her eyes, she struggled to block the rasp of terry cloth over skin.

"I feel much better now."

"Good." She reached for the door. "I'll be in the kitchen."

"Do you have a robe or something I could borrow?"

She couldn't say what possessed her at that moment, but some errant female chromosome had her whirling around to stare at him.

Miles and miles of tanned flesh stretched over well defined muscle, marred only by another of those skimpy towels she'd bought at the dollar store, greeted her.

He smiled wanly. "I'll have to figure something out on the clothes."

She definitely should have left him on the side of that road.

Now, no matter what she did, that incredible image would be forever burned onto her retinas.

Chapter Seven

Keith paced the living room of Ashley Orrick's small home, pausing once every few minutes to peek out the window for the anticipated delivery. The messenger should be there any time now. He glanced at the digital read out on the television's cable box: 11:15 p.m.

He verified again that the kitchen and rear door were secure before moving into the short hall to check her room. She'd gone to bed half an hour ago. He'd insisted she leave the door open. She didn't like it, but she gave in when faced with his unyielding determination.

She hadn't moved a muscle as far as he could tell. Still sleeping soundly.

At least she looked as if she was asleep. But he didn't trust her so he assumed nothing.

He'd never met a more resourceful woman.

He leaned against the doorjamb, let the light that stretched into the hall from the living room fall softly across her face and watched the steady rise and fall of her chest. She'd kept a vehicle hidden in a remote location for a quick getaway in the event she was made. He wondered how many gas stations along how many routes she had scouted to ensure she could escape from a variety of locations. She appeared to know every tree and trail in those woods off the interstate.

Absolutely amazing.

He wouldn't even hazard to guess how many other escape routes she had around the town she had called home for the past year.

It took a hell of a lot of motivation to go to those lengths to protect herself and the location of her child. That alone made him wonder about Desmond Van Valkenberg. Could he be the monster Ashley Orrick and her mother thought him to be?

Still, the man was dying. Whatever kind of boyfriend he'd been ten years ago, didn't he deserve the opportunity to know his only child?

Tough questions. But it wasn't his job to analyze whatever motivated this woman or the man who was his client. He couldn't get caught up in whatever old battles these two waged.

Finding the boy was his number one priority. During the past two hours, he'd searched the house, other than her bedroom, from top to bottom. He'd found nothing. If she wouldn't give up his location, then he was to turn her or her location over to Van Valkenberg's people.

His conscience nagged him.

What if turning her over to Brody or Van Valkenberg was a mistake?

Keith kicked the idea out of his thoughts and headed back into the living room. He couldn't let sympathy get in the way of doing his job. The researcher in him didn't want to ignore the details and that was his problem. He had to get past it. His orders were clear.

The Colby Agency didn't work for monsters. If Victoria thought Van Valkenberg was on the up-and-up, then he was. It was as simple as that.

He traced the small bandage he'd taped onto his forehead. The gash wasn't that bad, maybe could have used one stitch. It had bled considerably, as head injuries will, but it wasn't so bad. He felt better now.

A light rap on the front door alerted him to the messenger's arrival. Since he was no longer armed, he checked first just to make sure it wasn't one of Ashley's escape plans. He'd already learned her neighbors looked out for her. There was no way to guess who else she'd recruited.

Ben Haygood stood on the porch. Despite the warm July night, he wore a suit as well as a trench coat and Bogart-style fedora. He looked exactly like a P.I. from the Fifties, or maybe a gangster. Smiling, he gave Keith a little wave when he spotted him taking a look out one of the front windows. Keith ducked away as if he'd been caught by the enemy. It might not have been subtle, but it wasn't as if he'd had any other way to verify who was out there. The front door didn't have one of those nifty peepholes.

Keith opened the door and ushered Ben inside. "You didn't have to come all this way yourself," he said quietly. He'd expected someone a lot lower in the pecking order and a lot less eccentric.

Ben shrugged his trench coat-clad shoulders. "I didn't mind. It was kind of cool taking the agency jet." A frown tugged his eyebrows together as he perused Keith's attire. "Nice robe."

Keith snatched the overnight bag Ben carried from him. "You tell anybody about this and—"

Ben held up a hand. "Don't worry. I won't say a word. We picked up your rental." He passed the keys to Keith. "It was right where you left it. Nothing appeared to have been bothered. The woman's—" he glanced around the room "—bag was still in the back seat. I left it there. The rental's parked in the driveway behind that beat-up sedan she drives."

"Thanks, Ben, I owe you." Keith opened the bag and found two changes of clothes, jeans and a shirt, as well as a pair of trousers, another shirt and a coordinating tie. Sneakers and loafers and all the other necessary items Keith had asked for. Ben prided himself on being thorough. "Looks like everything is here."

Ben passed him a large envelope next. "You'll need this, as well."

Keith looked confused a moment, then opened the envelope. A new agency ID and credit card were inside. A cell phone, pocket PC and, unbelievably, a new Illinois driver's license.

"How did you manage this?" He checked out both sides of the license and it looked like the real deal.

With a knowing grin on his face, Ben said, "I can't divulge that little secret." He looked around covertly and added in a near whisper, "Besides, you wouldn't want to know. Trust me. One word of advice, though. Get the real thing as soon as you get back to the city. Your average cop won't know the difference, but if he calls it in…"

"I gotcha." He'd just take the guy's word for it. "Thanks. This'll help a lot."

Ben shoved his hands into the pockets of his trench coat. "I should get going."

Keith was just about to ask him if he'd forgotten something when Ben hesitated, looked a little uncertain of himself, then patted the left side of his coat. "Oh yeah," he said with a laugh, "I almost forgot." He reached into an interior pocket of his coat and dragged out a .38 in a clip-on holster. "You might need this."

Keith took the gun, no longer reluctant to feel the weight of a deadly weapon in his hand. "After running into those thugs in the woods, I can see why carrying a weapon is necessary." No one would have to twist his arm in the future where being armed was concerned. He never had been big on guns, but that attitude had just changed drastically in the past twenty-four hours.

"So, how's it going otherwise?" Ben asked, one hand on the doorknob. He glanced toward the hall that led to Ashley's bedroom. "Is Miss Orrick giving you any unexpected trouble?"

"Nothing I can't handle." Was Ben checking up on him for the boss? Or was he simply nosy?

"Any idea where the kid is yet?"

Keith shook his head. "She's keeping that information to herself so far."

"Just curious about how close the age progression turned out." He opened the door. "I should get going. The pilot's expecting us back within the hour."

"Thanks again."

Keith watched from the window as Ben loaded into what looked like another rental. The driver would take him back to the airfield where the agency jet waited. He'd be back in Chicago in no time.

Keith wondered if he'd be getting back there anytime soon. Hopefully he would and with his first successful field assignment under his belt.

Letting the blind snap back into place, he turned his attention back to business. He grabbed the bag Ben had delivered and headed for the bathroom. He checked on Ashley before easing her bedroom door closed except for a narrow crack. If she got out of that bed, he wanted to know it; he also needed a moment's privacy to get changed into his own clothes. He'd trashed the suit he'd been wearing; there wasn't a dry cleaner in the world who could have salvaged it.

Another lesson learned. Never head out on an assignment, no matter how confident of its brevity, without a change of clothes and other essentials for everyday survival.

Not wasting any time, he stepped just inside the bathroom door, didn't close it all the way and dragged on the boxers, jeans and shirt. Clean socks and dry shoes were an immense relief. He shook his head when he discovered a wallet in the bag, as well. Ben definitely thought of everything. With a few other essentials out of the way, he reopened the door to Ashley's room and simultaneously turned to head back to the living room. He figured he could rest on the couch for a few hours, but sleep was out of the question.

As he turned to head in that direction, something in his peripheral vision captured his attention.

He'd looked in on her so many times tonight he'd memorized every detail of the way she was positioned in the bed. Something was different now. Just one big ball rolled up in the middle of the bed.

Dammit. He should never have let her out of his sight. That mound was likely her pillows and she was probably long gone.

Adrenaline charging through him, he burst into

her room and jerked the cover back to confirm his worst fears.

"What the hell are you doing?"

He froze. The lamp on the table next to the bed clicked on. Glaring furiously, she snatched the sheet out his hand. "Get out of my room!"

"Sorry." He backed away. Grimaced at the pain roiling through his skull that he hadn't noticed until now. Apparently, sudden moves were still off-limits.

She scrambled off the bed then and stood, hands on hips, to glare at him some more. "Look, I don't know why you're still hanging around. I'm not going to tell you where my son is. No way. Not tonight, not ever. So stop wasting both our time. You should get on that jet with your friend and go back to Chicago because I'm not cooperating."

The idea that she hadn't been asleep at all frustrated him further. "I could have done that," he snapped. "I could have dragged you on that plane with me and taken you right to Van Valkenberg's door."

She recoiled as if his words had burned her. "It won't do you or him any good to force me back against my will. I won't give up my son."

Part of him couldn't help feeling a little sorry for her. "There are laws against what you're doing, Miss Orrick," he reminded as gently as he could.

"There are laws against forcing a person across state lines, too, Mr. Devers."

She had him there. He couldn't actually take her back to Chicago unless she was willing to go. In fact, legally, she could throw him out of her private residence. All he had on his side was the likelihood that she didn't want trouble with the police.

What he needed was the boy's location. And he'd discovered not a trace of evidence anywhere on the premises to indicate she even had a son. Apparently getting her to disclose that information wasn't going to happen anytime soon.

"You're right." He reached into his pocket and withdrew his new cell phone. "I should just get this over with now and give your location to Van Valkenberg's people. I've done all I can."

She grabbed his arm. "No." The frustration and fury she'd displayed moments ago had been upstaged by fear. "I'll go back with you. Let's just get some sleep. We're both exhausted. I won't try anything. I promise."

Keith went on instant alert. The last time she'd behaved as if she intended to cooperate, she'd ditched him at a gas station. His gaze narrowed with mounting suspicion at her sudden about-face. "What're you up to this time?"

She held up both hands. "Nothing. I swear."

That move pulled the hem of the night shirt she wore a little farther up her thighs, drawing his wayward attention there. Great legs.

Her arms fell to her sides and one look at her face

told him she knew he'd been staring at her legs. But then, she would have to be blind not to notice. His frustration level ratcheted up a notch.

"I think we need some coffee," he suggested, attempting to find some place his gaze could rest that wouldn't distract him. The words *Dream Babe* were plastered across her chest. If he looked there, he'd get caught up in the shape of her breasts beneath the worn thin fabric. The contours of her face were no less absorbing. If he looked for more than a second or two, he'd just keep staring. "We need to talk."

"I have heat-and-serve cinnamon rolls," she offered cheerfully. Maybe too cheerfully.

"All right. Cinnamon rolls and coffee, and we'll discuss the issues."

She nodded eagerly.

He turned away but hesitated before leaving the room. "Maybe you should put some clothes on," he said without looking back.

She now fully understood that he had a problem with looking at her so scantily dressed. Probably wasn't in his best interest to have let that slip. It was just as well, he decided as he left her room, closing the door carefully behind him. If he kept getting sidetracked by various parts of her body, she'd notice anyway.

He glanced back at her door. He wasn't worried about her trying to slip out the windows. The two in her bedroom had been painted shut long ago. Just now, he needed that barrier between them.

Who knew? Maybe the building attraction would serve his purposes. He didn't see exactly how just yet, but he could hope.

HE WAS ATTRACTED to her.

Ashley stood in the middle of her bedroom, both stunned and flattered.

Okay, she shouldn't be flattered, but she just couldn't help it. She couldn't even remember the last time she'd thought about the concept, much less felt any electricity generated between her and a member of the opposite sex.

This private detective liked what he saw. Her heart fluttered. She'd stopped thinking of herself as desirable ages ago.

Stop it, she ordered herself. This was not the time to go there, as tempting as it might be. She chewed her lower lip and thought about the situation for a moment. She could use this to her advantage.

While his friend had visited, she'd used his distraction as an opportunity to put Plan B into action. Since she hadn't been able to give him the slip, and his determination on reuniting her with Desmond was clear, she'd had no choice but to assume the worst-situation scenario.

She'd called her mother on her land line. Always

a last resort for her as far as communications were concerned.

Now all she needed was forty-eight hours to make sure all was a go. Once forty-eight hours had passed, it wouldn't matter what Desmond or anyone else did to her; Desmond would never know where Jamie was.

Because even she wouldn't know.

Chapter Eight

The smell of cinnamon and fresh-brewed coffee had filled her kitchen before Ashley sat down with Keith Devers. What would it hurt to tell him as much of the truth as possible? It wasn't as if it would change anything. She'd already set things in motion. Nothing she or he or anyone else did would change that now.

She and her mother had made the decision long ago. If the time ever came when Ashley felt that there was no other way to protect her son, this extreme step would be taken. To ensure that her mother had sufficient time to escape, Ashley's job would be to distract the threat for as long as possible, hopefully for at least forty-eight hours.

The countdown had begun two hours ago.

She lifted the tray of cinnamon rolls out of her oven and inhaled deeply, memories of making sticky rolls like this with her son flooding her senses. Jamie loved the sugary sweet pastries and she loved baking them for him, especially from scratch. It had been a really long time since they'd baked pastries or cookies, much less anything else, together. Too long.

Using a spatula, she lifted a couple of rolls and slid them onto plates. She could feel Devers watching her. She'd purposely chosen her tightest jeans and a form-fitting pullover with a hemline that didn't quite reach the waist of her jeans to hopefully distract him further.

A tingle of excitement shimmered through her and she silently scolded herself for allowing such a foolish thought. She hadn't set out to tempt a man since her college days. She wasn't even sure she remembered how. But since she'd noticed him eyeing her feminine assets, she figured that was the route to go. Might as well use what she had.

He was quite the snazzy dresser himself. As she poured two mugs full of coffee, she stole a covert look at him. He had spent the past half hour alternating between peeking out the windows and leaning against the counter to observe her every move. Now he stood propped against the doorjamb, having just moved back to the kitchen from his routine round of the rest of the house. The jeans he wore fit nicely and looked well washed, as if maybe they were his favorite pair. The shirt was navy, an appealing contrast to the blue eyes. The shirttail was tucked in. A leather belt perfectly matched the loafers he wore.

Metro, she decided. The kind of guy who liked to

look good no matter what the setting or circumstances. Exceedingly well groomed and very particular about his wardrobe, but undeniably straight as the proverbial arrow when it came to his sexual preferences.

She barely caught herself before the smile slid across her lips. Unsure how long she could keep it to herself, she turned her attention back to serving the midnight snack she had prepared. The idea of how disgruntled he had looked in the woods with his clothes ripped and soiled had her grinning widely. She'd been a little too busy to notice how much the situation bothered him; then he'd gotten that blow to the head and that had changed everything. He'd bandaged the injury, which only made him look more appealing.

She couldn't like him. Certainly couldn't trust him. She had to remember that, no matter how much those feminine assets of hers kept noticing his masculine ones.

If they hadn't gotten captured by those drug hoodlums, she wouldn't be here right now trying to entertain the enemy and her son wouldn't be headed to who knows where with her mother.

"Is there something I can do to help?" he offered, his voice sounding even deeper than usual after the extended silence.

"I've got it." She placed the mugs on the table, one next to each plate. "Let's dig in," she invited as she took a seat at the table.

He sat down directly across from her, placed the paper napkin on his lap and dug in. Contrastingly, she kept her napkin clutched in her hand. Whenever she ate anything sticky like this, she always got messy. No point in sticking her napkin someplace that wasn't handy.

"Not too bad for ready-to-bake," she commented after swallowing half her roll practically in one bite.

He nodded and took another bite. That he had consumed his first roll with scarcely a pause told her he didn't have any complaints.

"How about another?" She jumped up to serve up another round without waiting for his answer.

"Why did you run away ten years ago?"

Well, they were supposed to talk. Too bad he'd decided to start all the way back at the beginning. There were parts she'd just as soon forget.

She slid into her seat again and considered how much to divulge. At first, she couldn't see how she had anything to lose by being truthful. Still, she wasn't sure about some aspects of her relationship with Desmond. Did this man know who he was dealing with? She didn't think so.

At least she hoped not. It would be a shame for a seemingly nice guy to knowingly represent such an evil man.

Only one way to find out what he knew. "I was afraid for my life."

He swallowed. "You've made that abundantly clear. My real question is what made you feel that way? Desmond Van Valkenberg is a highly respected businessman. He's never been associated with the slightest scandal. What do you feel he did that threatened you and your son?"

Ashley suppressed the anger that immediately rose at his dismissal of her assertions against Desmond. Like everyone else, Devers only saw what was on the surface. Gave Desmond the benefit of the doubt over her first-hand knowledge. Since she'd been the one to run, she was automatically considered the one who had something to hide...the one who'd done wrong.

It just wasn't fair. She couldn't change people's attitudes. She'd learned that eight years ago when Desmond had come after her the first time. He had the world charmed, mainly because of his father's longstanding reputation. Desmond used the memory of his father to his advantage. He had it all—money, power and respect. She was insignificant; her feelings carried no weight.

"He tried to kill me."

Devers looked surprised but then, she'd known he would. She had chosen that announcement for its shock value.

"He hurt you physically?"

She had fully expected the skepticism she saw in

those blue eyes, damn him, but what she hadn't anticipated was the other thing just beneath. Disapproval or something on that order. The question was, did he disapprove of her charges against Desmond or her period?

"Yes. Not in the usual fashion," she hastened to add. "It was more subtle, at least until the bitter end."

The skepticism nudged out the other emotion she'd noted in his eyes. "In what way?"

Why bother? He wasn't going to believe anything she said anyway.

But she had to try, had to keep him distracted. Ultimately she knew she would end up in Chicago facing Desmond, but she needed to put that off as long as possible.

"At first it was indifference. He was gone most of the time during the second half of my pregnancy. I had no one but his minions for support of any kind. I found out later that he indulged himself by having numerous affairs during that time."

Devers finished off his coffee, set the mug aside and managed an expression devoid of emotion. "Were you able to confirm the affairs?"

"I saw the videotapes." Maybe she shouldn't have been so smug about that answer. She'd set herself up for the question she knew would follow.

"You hired a private detective to follow him? Is that how you got videos of his indiscretions?"

The disapproval was back. Whatever else he thought she couldn't read, but his distaste for her story was abundantly clear. The idea that he perhaps considered her somehow unsavory because of something Desmond had done made her all the more furious.

"No." She squeezed her lids closed for a moment or two to regain her composure. She'd snapped, hadn't meant to. This was a sore subject for her. "Taping his sexual encounters is—or at least was—a hobby of Desmond's." Her lips tightened again at the thought. "He didn't like it when I discovered his little sideline."

"You're certain he would have hurt you physically had you stayed?"

Ashley sipped her coffee, working hard to keep her frustration at a manageable level. "No, he wouldn't have hurt me. He would have killed me."

"Just because you discovered his failure to remain monogamous?"

"Isn't that enough?" Incensed that he could analyze the situation with such unemotional logic, she shoved back her chair and stood. "Maybe it doesn't bother you when your significant other cheats on you, but I had a problem with it."

He stood, picked up his plate and mug. "So you got jealous and angry and you left."

Ashley drew in a deep, determined breath. *Stay calm. Don't screw this up.* "I left because I was afraid for my safety and my child's."

She turned, her movements mechanical, and walked to the sink. She rinsed her plate and tucked it into the dishwasher. Devers rinsed his plate and passed it to her. He refilled his mug and gestured to hers with the carafe. "More coffee?"

"No, thank you." She marched back to the table and sat down. A quick glance at the clock told her it was 1:45 a.m. This was going to be a long night.

"What made you fear for you son's safety?" he asked when he resumed his seat directly across from her.

She lifted her shoulders in a pointed shrug. "I don't know maybe it was the way he put a pillow over a helpless three-month-old in his bassinet to muffle his crying."

Now that got his attention. "You're sure it wasn't an accident?"

Ashley shook her head. This guy was incredible. "The bassinet was all the way across the master bedroom from our bed. Have you seen his house? It was a very large room. The pillow didn't just walk over there and lay itself on top of my baby."

The grim expression that claimed his face then gave her some sense of satisfaction.

"Had he been drinking? Drugs, maybe?"

She made a sound of disbelief. What was wrong with this guy? Was he dense? "You should get to know your client better, Mr. Devers. Desmond doesn't do any sort of drugs, he gets his highs in other ways." A chill went through her as memories bombarded her. All those women he'd sexually abused. He was sick, that was what he was. Sick and demented.

"You have to understand, Miss Orrick," he explained calmly, "I can only base my perceptions on Mr. Van Valkenberg's current reputation. The fact is, his past reputation is unblemished, as well. He's a pillar of the community, so to speak. It's difficult to balance that image with the one you're outlining for me here."

She couldn't do this. "You know." She stood. "Think what you will." She shoved her chair under the table and stormed to her bedroom. It was two in the morning. She needed sleep and distance.

When daylight came, she'd just have to figure out some other way to distract the guy. She'd had enough for tonight.

Part of her would love to just get this over with. Get into that rented sedan of his and drive straight back to Chicago to face the monster she'd been running from all this time. It would feel so good to show him that he couldn't win.

But she couldn't do that. She had to wait. She had to be sure that enough time had passed to facilitate her mother's part in this desperate plan. If Desmond discovered that she couldn't tell him where their son was, he would move heaven and earth to find her mother and Jamie. To prevent any possibility of his success, Ashley had to ensure that her mother and son were well out of reach.

Forty-four more hours. Not a minute less.

KEITH WINCED at the sound of Ashley Orrick's bedroom door slamming hard against the frame.

He hadn't expected her to get so upset. His questions had seemed logical to him. He hadn't been refuting her claims; rather he'd requested further clarification. Surely she realized that he needed to understand the situation fully in order to come to any conclusions.

And then what?

He stowed his empty coffee mug in the dishwasher. His assignment had nothing to do with Van Valkenberg's domestic troubles, real or imagined.

Still, the idea that the guy was some sort of pervert gave him second thoughts. It didn't seem right to usher a child into a situation like that.

Then again, he was only getting one side of the story. Van Valkenberg wasn't here to defend himself.

Yet, why would Ashley bother lying?

He walked slowly toward the door that separated them. What did she have to gain by making up all these stories? It didn't make sense.

Rich guys like Van Valkenberg had to worry about parasites draining them of money. The man's representative had put Ashley Orrick squarely in that category.

If that was the case, why didn't she just go for the

money? It wasn't as if Van Valkenberg wanted to take her child from her; he simply wanted visitation rights. It was all outlined in the legal documents Keith had given her mother.

He rapped on the door. "You'll need to leave this open." He braced for her fury.

The door swung inward. "Why don't you just sleep in here with me and then you won't have to worry."

He knew she was madder than hell and hadn't meant her remark to come out the way it sounded. But saying it out loud put the idea in his head and, frankly, he had a damned difficult time evicting the thought.

"That won't be necessary, Miss Orrick, but I would prefer that you keep the door open."

She ran her fingers through all that rich auburn hair. The movement drew her blouse up higher on her midriff and he couldn't help but notice.

"Look," she said, drawing his gaze back to her face which wasn't much help in getting his mind back on business, "we're both exhausted. Your head has to still ache. Why don't we just get some sleep? I'm sure we can discuss all of this with clearer heads tomorrow."

She was right. Though his head wasn't exactly hurting, it was sore and felt like a lead weight attached to his shoulders. Thankfully, the nausea and dizziness were history.

"I agree. We'll get some sleep and we'll talk on the way back to Chicago. Your story has me thinking it might be necessary to contact my superior and take a second look at the situation."

Astonishment stole over her and she stood there facing him with those lush lips parted in shock.

"Did you think I wasn't listening?" he asked. As much as he wanted the location of her son to complete his assignment, he couldn't be indifferent to her dilemma. Maybe he should, but he couldn't pretend that there wasn't something there. The woman was terrified of the idea of letting Van Valkenberg get his hands on her son.

"I…" She wet her lips and his mouth went dry. "I guess I'm surprised that you would even care."

Her words were like a slap in the face. He'd been accused of a lot of things in the past, such as being obsessive about details or being in his own little world, but not once in his life had he been accused of not caring about other people's problems when they were right in front of him.

She smiled faintly. "I guess you're the one who's surprised now."

He took a big mental step back. He'd overstepped professional bounds here. "We should call it a night." It was a cop-out, but what the hell. This was a no-win scenario. Anything he said would only drag him deeper into forbidden territory.

She gave him her back and strode toward her bed, pulling her blouse over her head as she went.

He blinked. Stepped back from the door just as her hands lit on the waist of her jeans and started to scoot them off her hips.

After executing a hard right, he put one foot in front of the other until he'd made his way to the couch.

Okay, so she'd made her point. Open bedroom doors were asking for trouble.

He dropped onto the sagging couch, kicked off his loafers and stretched out. She needed a new sofa. This thing was a wreck, from its tattered upholstery to its broken-down springs.

It would do in a pinch, he supposed. He needed sleep for sure. All he had to do was get the picture of her half-naked body out of his mind. The light from the hall had provided precisely enough illumination to make sure he didn't miss a single curve of all that creamy skin. The way her torso narrowed into that tiny waist made him want to mold his hands along every soft inch.

She'd done that on purpose, to prove her point and to get under his skin. He couldn't let her do that. She was a desperate woman, determined to keep her child away from his father. She might very well be capable of most anything, driving him crazy with lust included.

To distract him.

He sat straight up.

She didn't have any plans to sleep. His lips formed

a grim line. Not this woman. She thought she had him mollified with her talk of abuse and little striptease act. No way. She had giving him the slip on her mind. He would fall asleep and she'd be out of here.

Absolutely no way was he letting her fool him again.

He got up, surveyed the room and picked out the tattered recliner. The leather was worn almost through in places, but it would do just fine.

With a quick look underneath to make sure it was safe to do so, he pushed the bulky piece of furniture across the hardwood floor of the living room and into the hall right in front of her bedroom.

He plopped into it and reclined. Perfect. Now, if she left that room, she'd have to climb over him. He'd already checked the windows. No way would she be getting one of those open without a toolbox and applying some major elbow grease.

She rose up in her bed; the light from the hall fell softly across her face highlighting her look of annoyance.

"I wasn't going anywhere."

He shot her a smile, then relaxed into the shabby leather and closed his eyes. "Well, now we'll both sleep better, 'cause I'm not going anywhere, either."

She plopped back down on her pillows, muttered something like *jerk*.

His lips stretched into another smile. Two could play this game.

She'd have to get up pretty early in the morning to get ahead of him two times in a row.

"I have a question for you, Mr. Devers."

Keith's eyes reluctantly opened. He blinked. He really should turn off the overhead light in the hall. Maybe leave the bathroom light on with the door partially closed. Just enough illumination to keep an eye on her.

"Sure. Ask away."

He let the footrest down and got up to make the change in the lighting.

The light in the hall went out with a flick of a switch. He reached for the one in the bathroom next.

"Have you ever been so afraid of something that you'd be willing to do anything to make sure it didn't happen?"

He stilled, his fingers on the switch. He didn't know why he hesitated; he should have flipped the switch upward to put some light on the situation. But her words kept him still, made him hesitate to do anything that might shatter the moment.

"I know you don't want to believe me," she said softly, her voice carrying in the darkness, gently caressing his senses. "But I swear to you that everything I've told you is the truth."

His heart pounded in time with the tension rushing through his body.

"If you'll give me the chance I can prove it."

He closed his eyes and drew in a breath to clear his head. He had to stop letting her get to him like this.

"I have evidence."

His eyes snapped open. Still, he didn't turn on the light.

"All you have to do," she urged, her voice tugging at him, "is give me twenty-four hours."

The rustling of sheets sent his tension to a whole new level. The pad of bare feet whispered in the darkness next. He could turn on the light…he could ask her what she was doing.

But he didn't.

She scooted the recliner out of the way enough to move into position directly in front of him. He could vaguely make out her form in the darkness. A light over the kitchen sink filtered into the living room, preventing the adjoining hall from being pitch-black.

"Can you do that? Give me twenty-four hours?"

Then he made his second mistake since taking this assignment. "All right. Twenty-four hours." He cursed himself for sounding breathless. She was toying with him here, and he knew it. He just didn't seem to be able to do anything about it.

"Thanks."

And then she made her first mistake.

She went up on tiptoe and kissed him on the cheek.

He felt her tremble as she drew away.

Keith wasn't the only one swimming against the tide here. He just hoped like hell he could outswim this foolish temptation.

Chapter Nine

At 8:30 a.m., Ashley grabbed her overnight bag from where she'd stashed it between the bed and the window.

She had to hurry. It was almost time.

Devers had already reported in to his superiors. She'd listened in as best she could. He'd told someone named Victoria that he anticipated new information in twenty-four hours.

She could hear him now checking the back door and anything else he felt needed to be locked or turned off in anticipation of their departure.

Ashley grabbed a pair of hiking boots, a flashlight, a bottle of aspirin, a compass and a couple of bottles of water from her stash in her closet. It took a little rummaging around to find the other item she needed. She tossed the articles into her bag and zipped it up. She bit her lower lip to restrain a smile. Her plan had worked. Now she just needed to make her final move.

Right…about…now.

Devers's cell phone rang.

She strolled into the living room with her bag in hand. "You ready?"

He looked puzzled by his call.

Another smile tickled her lips, but Ashley held it back. "I'm going to put this in the car." She pointed to her bag.

"Yes, I know who you are," he said to the caller. He held up a hand to Ashley.

She pretended not to see it and headed for the door.

Still talking on his phone he followed her onto the porch, determined to keep her in sight.

Ashley held out her hand for the keys to his rental. He hesitated at first, looked from her to the car parked only a few feet away from where they stood, then dragged the keys from his pocket.

She snagged them from his palm and bounded down the steps to the car's trunk. She shook off the little shiver that touching his hand had generated.

Stop it, she ordered herself.

That stupid kiss she'd left on his cheek had haunted her all night.

Smooth move, Ash, she mused.

Opening the trunk, she peeked around the rising lid to make sure he wasn't coming any closer. He'd followed her as far as the bottom of the steps. Apparently he felt safe with watching her from there. She glanced at her own car parked parallel to and on the left of his. She listened intently to make sure he was still a few feet away. As long as he didn't move this could work.

Holding her breath, she set her bag into the trunk next to Devers's and reached for the tire wrench lying in plain sight next to the spare tire. She started to shove it into the bag with her stuff but opted to put it in his instead. He'd be less likely to check his own bag. Hurrying as fast as she could, she tucked it beneath his suit and quickly zipped the bag closed. Grabbing the bottle of aspirin and the one other item necessary for this stage of her plan, she zipped her bag again and moved around to the driver's side of the car.

With a quick look to ensure Devers was still occupied, she yanked the rear door open and rummaged around until she found her cosmetic bag in the overnight satchel she'd left in the car the day before yesterday. She stuffed the two items into the small bag of essentials and hastily closed things up before hefting the overnight bag out of the car.

When she turned around, Devers was standing right behind her. He was still on the phone.

The breath she'd been holding rushed out of her lungs.

He took the bag from her hand, moved to the trunk, tossed it inside next to the others and slammed the lid shut all in one fluid motion.

"Thank you for calling." Devers closed his phone

and slid it back into his shirt pocket. "I locked the front door. We should get going." He pulled the directions she had written down for him out of his back pocket.

She nodded, still unable to slow her heart's frantic beating.

When they'd both settled into the car and he'd briefly reviewed her directions, he started the engine and backed out of her drive.

Ashley stared at the place that had been her home for the past year and she couldn't help feeling a little sentimental. She wouldn't be back here.

Not that the place was so great.

She'd been lonely here. More than ever before. She'd missed her son so badly.

She'd missed human touch, period.

Ten years was a long time.

Looking out the window, she let the self-pity she usually kept locked away slip into conscious thought.

Once, about three years after she'd left Desmond, she'd met someone. They'd talked, really enjoyed each other's company. But then he'd started to ask questions. That had ruined everything. He just couldn't understand why she was so evasive.

The trouble was, she considered as she looked back, he had been a sincerely nice guy. He'd wanted a relationship, not just recreational sex.

Relationships were off-limits for her. No ties whatsoever.

She'd studied everything available in books and on the Internet regarding how to disappear. She knew a million tricks to lose herself, to evade being caught. And how to escape a captor.

The one thing she couldn't escape was the loneliness.

No matter how she pretended, she couldn't make it go away. God knows she'd tried.

She was still fairly young and healthy. Reading books and watching movies only went so far when it came to fulfilling her needs. Even a close female friend with whom to simply talk was pretty much out of the question. Sure, she talked to Gina once in a while and to Marla when she visited Jamie, but that wasn't the same as someone she could turn to on a moment's notice.

Guilt barbed her. Gina and Marla were the best friends anyone, male or female, could hope for. She was blessed to have them looking out for her and her son. That was a given.

This blue funk wasn't really about her friends. She was just lonely, that was all. She longed to be held by strong arms. To be treated like a woman...touched like a woman.

By a man.

Her gaze slid to the only man around, her driver and captor.

There was a little bit of attraction going on

between them. No denying that. But nothing could come of it. He had been hired by the man who would like nothing better than to see her dead.

She wondered if telling this man that she feared for her life was a mistake. Again, that familiar feeling of desperation had played into her decision. She needed time and this had been the only way she could think of to fool this guy. Maybe *fooling him* wasn't the right expression. She needed to keep him *distracted* a little while longer.

That was the best she could hope for. Keep him distracted and following a dead lead until her mother and son were out of harm's way.

No one could touch her baby then.

SHE WAITED for an hour.

It felt like two.

But she wanted to ensure they were well into no-man's-land. An area miles from nowhere. Lots of roads in the area fit that description but this one in particular was even more remote. They didn't call Ft. Leonard Wood "Ft. Lost in the Woods" for nothing.

Even more important, for the next ten miles or so, it was pretty much a dead zone. It was almost impossible to get cell phone service.

She was counting on that more than she preferred to admit.

For the last five minutes, she'd been rubbing her forehead. He'd noticed.

"Do you mind stopping to let me get some aspirin out of my bag? I have a horrendous headache."

He sent a sideways glance in her direction. "You have something to drink?"

"Bottled water in my bag. You want some?"

He shook his head. "I could stretch my legs, I guess."

Ashley tensed. His getting out could make her next move trickier.

The tires bumped over the grass as he eased onto the shoulder of the road. After shoving the gearshift into Park, he got out. She did the same. He met her at the trunk and unlocked it.

"Thanks." She managed a tight smile.

He nodded once.

She leaned deep into the trunk and fished around for her cosmetic bag and then a bottle of water. He watched her every move. Her pulse pounded.

Did he have to hover?

When she stepped back from the trunk, he shut the lid and moved back around to the driver's side.

For a second, she couldn't decide what to do.

Then inspiration struck.

She covertly unzipped her cosmetic bag and strode toward the front passenger door. Just as she reached it she dropped her bag.

"Damn." She looked through the glass at the waiting driver. "Just a minute."

Her fingers trembling, she grabbed the small wrench used for loosening or tightening the air valves on tires. She snatched off the valve's small top, shoved the wrench into place and gave it one full turn. Then she tossed it under the car.

A foot settled onto the asphalt on the other side of the car. From her position on her hands and knees her gaze riveted to that loafer-clad foot.

She grabbed the rest of her stuff and shot to her feet. "Sorry."

Devers studied her suspiciously from across the top of the car, but he didn't say anything, just got back behind the wheel.

Ashley got back into her seat and dragged on the safety belt. That he hadn't started the car and put it into gear to head out again made her heart slam unmercifully against her ribcage.

She looked at him, praying he couldn't see the panic in her eyes. "What's the holdup?"

He shrugged. "Thought I'd let you take your aspirin before I pulled back onto the road."

Dredging up an annoyed voice, she huffed, "You're wasting time, Devers. Let's go."

Looking flustered, he cranked the engine, pulled the gearshift into Drive and eased back onto the road.

Seeing her act all the way through, she popped a

couple of aspirins into her mouth and chugged the water. In an effort to keep busy, she rearranged all her stuff in the cosmetic bag and zipped it closed. She sat it on the seat between her and Keith. If he tried to accuse her of anything later, he wouldn't find any evidence in her bag.

Don't look at him, she told herself. *Keep your eyes straight ahead.*

No, close your eyes.

She closed her eyes and leaned back against the head rest. If she had a headache, she would do that. Right? Okay. Relax.

The minutes ticked by.

Had she done something wrong?

Should she have turned it twice instead of once?

"What now?" he grumbled.

The car had started to ride a little rougher than before. Ashley opened her eyes and looked around. "What's wrong?"

Devers shook his head and swore softly. "Feels like we've got a flat."

Goose bumps tumbled over her skin. "There's a spare, right?" She blinked, giving him her most innocent expression.

"Yeah, sure."

He guided the car onto the side of the road once more. She ordered her fingers to stay still. She fluctuated between wanting to curl and flex them and wanting to tuck them under her arms.

When he opened his door, she asked, "Do you need me to help?"

Those blue eyes nailed her to the spot. "Stay in the car. I don't need to have to worry about what you're doing while I handle this."

"Okay."

She heard the slap of shoe leather on asphalt and then the pop of the trunk. Her nerves jangled with each sound.

The shuffle of bags.

A couple of hot curses.

She knotted her hands together.

If he figured out she'd had something to do with this, he might just go ballistic. A surge of fear sent her pulse racing. Okay, she should have thought of that. So far as she could tell, Devers appeared to be a nice guy. She felt reasonably sure he wouldn't do anything crazy.

More shuffling in the trunk.

The thud of bags hitting the ground.

Now he was ticked off.

The back door opened. She tensed.

What would she do under normal circumstances? If she hadn't sabotaged the tire herself?

She unfastened her safety belt and turned around in the seat. "What're you doing? I thought you said we had a flat. Don't you know how to change a flat tire?"

When his gaze met hers, she knew there would be no getting out of the fact that she was a suspect in his latest dilemma.

"What did you do, Ashley?"

Her breath caught. Partially from his fierce glare and, as much as she hated to admit it, partly from his use of her first name.

"What're you talking about?" she said, summoning up a properly offended expression.

He shook his head. "I should have known you were up to something."

He prowled under the seats. Swore some more. Nothing particularly offensive. She turned back around and plopped back into her seat, mostly so she wouldn't smile where he could see her.

The back door slammed and she watched from the corner of her eye as he walked back to the flat tire and then kicked it as hard as he could.

"That had to hurt," she muttered, trying hard not to laugh.

Then she held her breath as he pulled out his cell phone and punched in a number.

AAA? Air support from his friend with the trench coat?

Just don't let there be any service where he was standing. She crossed her fingers and watched, still afraid to breathe.

His lips compressed into a thin line as he obviously stabbed the End Call button and entered another one. He did this five or six times before he admitted defeat.

He looked at her through the windshield and she realized that he knew she was somehow responsible for this latest run of bad luck.

Time to perform a little damage control.

She hoisted the door open and got out. "What is it now?"

Judging by his accusing stare, he wasn't buying her innocence at all.

"We have a flat tire." He gestured to the tire. "We have no tire wrench." He waved his hand toward the trunk. Then he held up his cell phone. "No service. Imagine that."

She narrowed her gaze. "Why does it feel like you're blaming me for this?"

He shoved the phone into the back pocket of his jeans. Her attention momentarily fixed on his well-formed buttocks.

The deep, rich sound of his laughter hauled her gaze from his nice buns to his equally nice face.

"You are good, lady."

Careful to keep that how-dare-you posture in place, she challenged, "Exactly what are you implying?"

"The whole I've-got-a-headache thing." He set his hands at his waist and locked his gaze with hers. "You did this. You dropped your stuff on purpose and then you did this." He flung his hands in the direction of the tire.

She stepped close and peered at the tire. "How was I supposed to have accomplished this act of sabotage?"

He moved his hands back and forth in front of him. "Oh, no. I'm not buying this innocent act." His frustration amped up a couple of notches. "Which way do we start walking to reach a service station or land line first?"

Ashley walked out into the middle of the road and looked first left and then right, taking her time as if weighing their options.

"Well." She pointed in the direction they'd come. "About fifty miles in that direction." She turned to look the other way. "At least that far in this direction."

He joined her in the road and did a three-sixty turn. "You don't know some shortcut through the woods?"

She moved her shoulders up and down. "Afraid not."

"No car hidden in the bushes." He wheeled on her then. "Wait. Maybe you've got a helicopter hidden around here somewhere."

So he was mad. He'd just have to get over it.

"I guess we should start walking." She looked at him expectantly. "Which way?"

He pointed the way they'd come. "At least I know what's back there."

"Whatever." She hustled over to the trunk and grabbed her overnight bag. On second thought, she took the bottle of water from the bag she'd packed this morning and decided getting the half bottle she'd left in the front seat wouldn't be a bad idea, either. They would need water before they got back to town.

Hours. She bit back a smile. The chances of a car coming along anytime soon was about the same odds as winning the lottery. This was the off road of off roads. Thank God this guy wasn't from anywhere near here.

She hefted the bag onto her shoulder and started to shut the trunk, but he stopped her. She jumped, surprised that he'd sneaked up on her like that.

"Might as well take mine, too. Just in case," he added with another one of those suspicious looks in her direction.

"Too bad you don't have any tricks in your bag." She knew she was tempting fate, but she just couldn't resist. He had the key to averting the long walk ahead right there in that bag; he just didn't know it.

He slammed the trunk lid shut. "You'd be surprised at what I have in this bag, Miss Orrick."

She smiled widely for him. "If you were a race horse, *Mr. Devers,* I wouldn't bet on you."

That pretty much took the wind out of his sails. He didn't have anything to say after that.

Or maybe it was the fact that she plopped her bag onto the closed trunk and fished out her sunblock that really peeved him. When she'd covered all exposed skin, she tossed the bottle to him. "It's going to get hot today." She glanced around. "I can feel it already."

When he didn't argue with her about the sunscreen, she figured he'd pretty much resigned himself to the idea that they would be walking all day. Feeling a little guilty for being so hard on him, she offered him the unopened bottle of water when he returned the protective lotion. He passed.

Guys. She gave her head a little shake. They always had to prove they were tougher.

Thank goodness they weren't smarter.

She glanced at the bag he'd thrown over his shoulder.

If he only knew…

Chapter Ten

The rain had been coming down for hours.

Keith estimated they were traveling about one mile every seventeen minutes, but he couldn't be precise about his calculations.

He looked at his watch again: 4:15. If his calculations were close, they had likely covered about twenty miles.

Only thirty to go.

He glanced at his companion.

She was soaked to the bone, as he was.

The major difference was the way her clothes had become glued to her body.

He tried hard not to notice. He really did.

Impossible.

From the corner of his eyes he watched her march forward. Determined. Resourceful. Highly imaginative. He had no idea how she'd managed to do what she did to the tire, but every instinct screamed at him that this was her doing. He simply had no proof.

Unfortunately that wasn't the trouble just now. At the moment, his major issue with the circumstances was the precise way her clothes had seemingly melted against her skin. Molded to her breasts. Plastered against her flat abdomen.

He wasn't usually so taken with belly buttons, but hers kept drawing his gaze to that place just above the snap on her jeans. It was a pleasant journey down the length of those drenched jeans. Already tight, getting wet gave them the appearance of a second skin.

"It's not nice to stare, Mr. Devers." She arrowed him a sidelong glance.

"I was just thinking," he said quickly, attempting to cover for his gawking. "You never told me exactly why you felt Van Valkenberg wanted you dead."

She pointed her gaze straight ahead once more but not before he noted the uncertainty in her eyes.

"We don't have to talk about him if you don't want to." He moved his soggy shoulders up and down. "I just thought maybe you wanted to give me more information about your side of things. That phone call I got before we left your house was from your friend, Gina."

Ashley tried to look surprised. "Really?"

"She wanted me to know that if I didn't believe you I'd get you killed."

"I'm sure that swayed your opinion," she said dryly.

"Just made me want to hear your side of things all the more."

"Why?" She glowered at him. "So you can pass the time? I don't think so. You work for him. Nothing I say is going to make any difference."

Did she really believe that?

"Wait a minute." Keith stopped.

She didn't. Not right away. Three steps in front of him, she finally relented and turned back to him. "What? It's raining, in case you haven't noticed." She performed a quick perusal of his waterlogged frame and he was pretty sure a hint of approval flashed in her eyes.

"I told you I'd refrain from making any conclusions until after I'd seen your evidence. What else do you want? I'd say that's more than going the distance."

He was setting aside his assignment in order to understand her hesitations. Bottom line, he was doing her a favor and this was the thanks he got.

She exhaled a big breath. "I guess you're right."

She started walking again. He fell into step next to her.

"I have this videotape."

Keith's senses went on elevated alert. He'd already decided that this was one smart cookie. If she had something on her ex-lover, it had to be the real thing. She was too smart to base everything on a trumped-up allegation.

Whether her assertions had any relevance to the present, and his assignment, was yet to be seen.

A minute or two of quiet passed with nothing but the sound of the rain drizzling down around them.

"He liked to play rough," she finally said. "At first, he was very kind and gentle with me. Especially during the early months of the pregnancy." She scrunched up her face as if she hated remembering this part of her past. "But after Jamie was born, things had changed. He hardly looked at me, much less touched me."

Somehow the thought of anyone touching her bothered Keith. He gave himself a mental kick for getting stupid and urged her to go on. "You said he hurt you."

She nodded. "Several times before I took off."

He focused his attention on the endless ribbon of highway and clamped his jaw shut to keep his comments to himself.

"Once he almost strangled me. He assured me it was a game and that he hadn't meant to hurt me. But I felt the way he fought to keep me from getting free. I knew he was lying."

Keith tried to rationalize her words. Could Van Valkenberg be that kind of sick bastard without anyone knowing?

"There were a lot of other women," she went on. "Mostly expensive hookers who knew how to keep secrets. He bragged that he never bothered with the same one twice."

Keith winced. "You had to be worried about what he was bringing home to you." The way diseases spread these days, that was a hell of a scary thought.

She still didn't look at him. "I was sick about it. For the first five years after I left, I got myself tested every six months. I almost lost my mind with worry. How would I take care of my son if I got sick?" She hugged her arms around herself.

Keith tamped down the urge to reach out to her and assure her everything was all right now. "But you were okay?"

She nodded. "I had myself tested again just a few months ago to be sure. Thank God he didn't screw me over that way, as well."

He barely caught the question before it was out of his mouth. It was none of his business if she'd been involved with anyone since. Considering what she'd been through, he surmised that she would have taken every precaution if that had been the case.

What the hell was he doing even going there?

Clearing sex from his mind, he ventured into the evidence she claimed to have hidden. "You feel that his proclivity for dangerous sex threatened your well-being, is that it? Do you have documented evidence of his…bizarre activities?"

He was fishing. She knew it. The look that knifed through the nasty weather left no question.

"The tape has him with a woman that his bizarre activities may have killed. I can't be sure, but I'm almost certain."

Taken aback by her revelation, he stopped, grabbed her by the elbow and pulled her around to face him. "You're telling me that you have evidence of a murder he committed?"

She looked away.

He sighed. "I didn't think so."

She jerked her arm free of his hold. "I have a tape of him with a woman who was reported missing two days later. When they finally found her body, she'd been murdered. Strangled to death. The same way he tried to strangle me." She touched her throat. "The assault that killed her was so vicious that bones were broken."

Not waiting for his response, she started forward again.

He stood there for a few moments, watched her walking away.

As uncertain as he was as to whether there could be any truth to her allegation, murder would certainly be strong enough motivation for her to have gone to all these lengths to hide.

But what if this was just another of her elaborate escape schemes?

Desmond Van Valkenberg was the agency's client. Keith owed his loyalty to him. Not to this woman who had reason to want to hide from her own past sins.

Within seconds, he'd caught up with her. He looked up at the sky as he did. Finally. The rain had stopped.

She peered up at the sky, as well. "Now we'll fry." She reached into her bag and came out with the sunblock again. "No point in taking any chances."

His patience way past an end, he waited until she'd coated her skin, then he followed her example. He already had a lump on his head. He didn't need any blistering to go along with it.

When they had walked another mile or so, he broached the subject that would no doubt be tender. "How much of his money did you take when you left?"

She didn't stop or look at him but he saw the way her jaw tightened at the question.

"I took only the money he had given me."

That was convenient. "How much was that?"

"A couple thousand. He'd given it to me to buy clothes. He didn't want me lounging around his mansion in anything I'd worn before the baby."

A frown worked its way across his forehead. "He was that domineering?"

She laughed. "You have no idea."

"Make me understand."

She stopped, causing him to stop, as well, and then she looked at him. Really looked at him.

"Every move I made was dictated by him. He told me what to wear. When to get up. Where to go. All aspects of my life were controlled by him."

Keith couldn't imagine living that way. "You never argued with him?"

She shook her head. "I was stupid."

"You were young," he offered, letting her off the hook.

"No," she countered. "I was stupid. So stupid that if I hadn't found out about the prostitutes and the murder, I would probably still be with him. Those dirty secrets of his put everything into perspective. I understood just how dangerous he was. I had to protect my son."

Then she walked off, leaving him to digest that profound revelation. She did a lot of that.

He started forward again, but made no move to catch up with her. "You loved him that much?"

She missed a step but didn't falter, kept right on walking.

He walked faster now, determined to have the answer to his question. "I asked if you loved him that much." He didn't know why it mattered, but it did.

Again she refused to look at him. "I thought I did. But maybe that was a lie, too."

His fingers curled around her right arm and tugged

her around to look at him again as they both drew to
a stop. "I have a feeling you don't do anything halfway,
lady. If you loved him, you loved him completely."

Her eyes shone too brightly and he wanted to kick
himself, literally, for putting those tears there.

"Then I guess I did. But that died a long time ago.
The only thing I want now is to keep my son away
from him." Her lips quivered and fury replaced the
softer emotions. "I don't want him anywhere near my
child. Ever."

Somehow, standing there dripping wet and
quaking with emotion, she looked so vulnerable that
he couldn't pretend not to care. He shrugged off his
bag and let it fall to the ground. Hers dropped right
next to his and he pulled her into his arms and held
her. Nothing else. Just held her tight for as long as
she wanted him to.

Not a car in sight, just pavement and trees as far
as the eye could see.

She leaned into him, let him hold her without resistance.

Strangely, it felt right.

IT WAS DARK when they reached the full-service
station he remembered passing some fifteen miles
outside Waynesville.

The guy was just closing up.

It took some talking and a hundred bucks on top

of the usual charge, but he agreed to take care of the flat tire right away.

"Do you have a clothes dryer around here?" Keith looked around the place and was relatively certain they were out of luck.

"Got one in my house trailer." He jerked his head toward the station. "I live round back. You're welcome to wait there, dry off, eat, whatever, while I take care of your car." He grinned. "For a fee."

Keith blew out a breath of frustration and gave the man another hundred.

He climbed into his work truck and peeled out of the parking lot. Keith took Ashley by the arm and guided her around behind the station.

Sure enough, a single wide mobile home, a rather small one that looked as if it had seen better days, stood waiting a dozen yards away.

Inside was far worse than the outside. Apparently the service station owner didn't have a wife or a maid.

Leaving Ashley in the tiny living room, Keith checked out the bathroom. He'd seen worse, but that wasn't saying much.

"You go first." He held the door open.

Ashley went into the bathroom and stripped off her wet clothes. Her feet and legs were numb with exhaustion. On second thought, maybe her whole body was numb. They had dried once, but then the rain had started again.

She dug out her dry clothes and quickly slipped into them. After dragging her brush through her hair, she realized she wasn't going to get out of this without using the less-than-sparkling facilities.

Having taken care of that necessary business, she turned the room over to Keith.

He gifted her with a brief smile as he stepped past her. Nice smile.

Keith. She didn't remember slipping into that informality. But she supposed when you told a guy about your former sex life, you needed to be informal.

She prowled around the kitchen and beyond until she discovered the clothes dryer in a closet in the hall leading to the home's one bedroom. She tossed her wet clothes into the dryer and set the timer.

Deciding that the dryer looked cleaner than anything else in the place, she slid up onto it and rested her weary bones.

The memory of how he'd held her flooded her mind, making her entire body tingle. She'd needed someone to do that for so long. She could scarcely believe that it was him, of all people. Some P.I. a madman had sent to bring her back to Chicago.

Vivid images of how he'd looked in those soaking wet clothes kept flashing one after the other in her mind. Sleek, muscled body. The man had to be an athlete. He was amazingly agile, too. And strong.

And handsome, that wicked voice she hadn't heard in more than a decade taunted.

Yes, he was all those things and way, way off-limits.

But, what if there was a chance that he would help her. He seemed disgusted by the things she'd told him about Desmond. Surely he wouldn't want to be responsible for forcing her back into that kind of situation.

He seemed to care.

She shivered as the feel of his strong arms around her invaded her senses all over again. Her eyes closed and for just a little while, she let herself relive those moments.

It had been so long, and she was so tired. She couldn't resist.

"I'll just toss my clothes in there with yours."

Her eyes flew open. He stood right in front of her, not a dozen inches away. She was usually so much better than this at staying on top of her surroundings.

"Sure." She propped her feet up on the washing machine so he could access the dryer's door.

He pitched his clothes inside and pushed the start button. The drum resumed turning beneath her and the heat radiated up, warming her bottom. She shifted, draping her legs back down in front of the dryer.

"We need to talk. Again."

She looked up just in time to see him coming

closer. Her heart stalled and any chance of breathing disappeared. He braced one hand on either side of her and looked deep into her eyes.

"You got one over me again."

Uh-oh. He'd found the tire wrench.

"I'm not sure what you're up to, Ashley."

There he went using her first name again. She refused to let him see her shiver, but it wasn't easy.

"From now on, we do things my way. You tell me exactly where we're going and I'll plot the route."

She grabbed her courage and yanked it up to where it should be. "Sorry, *Keith,* I can't do that."

"Why not?"

He didn't budge an inch. Kept his face right in front of hers. Too close. The rest of his body was as well.

"Because you're the enemy. You work for the man who wants my child. The same man who tried to kill me and who I'm certain has killed at least one woman. I can't do anything your way. Not willingly."

Those electric blue eyes grew suspicious. "How can I be sure this isn't just another one of your outlandish tricks?"

She looked straight into those eyes and let him see the truth in hers. "Because I need you to believe me and for that reason alone I'm willing to take a chance on you. But we have to do things my way."

He stared right back, analyzing, searching, attempting to see any hidden agenda. That she could live with, but when that mesmerizing gaze dropped to her lips, she lost her balance.

And she took a major risk.

She threw her arms around his neck and dragged his face those few inches so that she could kiss him square on the mouth.

He didn't resist. She had known he wouldn't. He let her lead. Let her kiss him until she felt ready to melt with the heat roaring through her body.

She let go. He drew back. And she dragged in an unsteady breath. "Seven years." She touched her lips, hardly believing she'd been so bold. "It's been seven years since I've been kissed like that."

"I think maybe another one is in order."

This time, he took charge. Took her face in his hands and drew her mouth up to this. His lips felt soft and firm at the same time. His palms against her cheeks made her want to feel those strong hands moving over her body, one slow inch at a time. She trembled. He kissed her harder.

She let her hands travel down his back, urging him closer. Before she realized what she was doing, she'd parted her thighs, allowing him even nearer.

He groaned, a sound that made her pulse leap. Made her squirm to be closer still.

He stopped.

His lips pulled away from hers, barely a breath

apart. For two fierce beats of her heart, he didn't move. Then he stepped away completely.

She felt cold and alone at his withdrawal.

"That shouldn't have happened," he murmured.

Whom was he trying to convince? Her or himself?

"But it did." She slid off the dryer, right back into his personal space. "Don't expect me to be sorry. I've waited a long time for that."

Before he could rally a response, she sidled past him and went back to the kitchen. She peeked into the fridge, grabbed a can of soda, the only thing she dared to touch. She searched the cupboards until she located a bag of chips.

At Keith's look of disapproval, she said, "He told us we could eat."

She opened the bag of chips and devoured a handful. She moaned in satisfaction. God, she'd been starving and she hadn't even realized it.

The fridge door slamming yanked her attention back to her companion. He'd gotten himself a soda, as well. She offered the bag of chips to him and he reached in for a handful.

While he munched on the chips, she searched for crackers and peanut butter. She would kill for some crackers and peanut butter.

"Yes!" She reached into the final cupboard and retrieved her bounty.

A few swipes of a clean butter knife later and she was in ecstasy. Food had never tasted so good.

When their feeding frenzy had slowed, she made an effort to clean up their part of the mess in the kitchen though she doubted the owner would notice the difference.

"You have peanut butter…" He swiped a place next to her mouth.

She swallowed at the lump that rose in her throat. "Got it."

Funny thing was, he hadn't stopped looking at her mouth.

"Thanks."

He nodded, his gaze still glued to her lips.

The front door burst open. "Got you folks fixed up." Damn.

Talk about bad timing. Or maybe she should consider herself saved by the intrusion.

"I can give you a lift back to your car," the mechanic offered.

Keith's gaze swung to him. "Don't tell me. For a *fee.*"

Chapter Eleven

The hum of the tires speeding along the dark pavement came close to lulling Ashley into sleep. Every time she got close, a burst of intense yearning would send off tiny explosions inside her. She tried to block the cause but it was impossible. He sat barely two feet away.

She refused to look at him again. Despite the darkness, the light from the dash gave off just enough of a glow for her to see his chiseled profile.

To make matters worse, the scent of him had seeped into the very pores of her skin. Any aftershave or cologne he'd splashed on the last time he showered had to be long gone. This was him. His skin and the rain and all those amazing male pheromones.

How she had missed that smell. She pressed her forehead against the cool glass of her window and restricted her gaze to the passing landscape. The scent of a man had never made her feel this way. There was something hypnotic about this man.

A shiver quivered through her.

That was the only explanation for her uncharacteristically bold behavior. The very idea that she'd kissed him. Not once, but twice. And the second time, holy smokes! She'd been acting like a sex-starved nympho.

Okay, truth be told, she was starved for a man's touch. Humiliation roiled through her at the idea that she'd admitted—out loud—that she hadn't been kissed in seven years. There was simply no other answer; she'd fallen under his spell big-time. Either that, or insanity had overtaken her temporarily.

That couldn't be it, she thought. *Temporary* by definition meant short-lived. This didn't feel as if it were fading one little bit. If anything, the attraction grew stronger, more complicated with each passing hour.

Being stuck in this car for hours wasn't helping. She needed some space. She huddled closer to her door. Distance. Anything to get him off her mind.

She closed her eyes and summoned a dozen mental pictures of her son. God, how she missed him. He and her mother would be well away from Missouri by now.

Then again, she couldn't be so sure they would leave Missouri. She had no idea what her mother's strategy included. That was the deal. Ashley couldn't know. Answers couldn't be gotten out of her if she didn't have them. Extreme maybe, but necessary in her opinion.

Her mind toyed with the idea that maybe Keith—she had to stop calling him by his first name—could help her. If she showed him her evidence, would he defect to her side? Forget about his commitments to the agency he worked for?

She was putting far too much stock into this brewing chemistry. But she had to try, didn't she? He seemed like a nice guy.

So had Desmond when you first met him, the voice of caution warned.

Appearances could be deceiving. She could only imagine how much Desmond was paying this agency to locate his son. Counting on this attraction to divert a man from his obligations to his career was not only foolish, but also outright dumb.

She might have been a fool once, but she wasn't going to be again. And she darned sure wasn't going to go stupid over a hot guy.

One look at the driver and her body staged a rebellion. A yearning so overpowering roared through her that she shook with it.

Sex, she assured the doubts nagging at her. She'd waited way too long and now she was suffering the consequences. If she'd had a healthy social life, she wouldn't be having this trouble keeping her mind off how it felt to be held in his arms. The incredible way he kissed. She looked away.

No use torturing herself.

This time was about distracting him. Sure, it would be nice if he believed her about Desmond being a monster, but the goal was to buy sufficient time for her mother and son.

As soon as she got out of this, she'd have to find a new life somewhere. Maybe California. She'd always wanted to live near the ocean. Someplace where the weather was nice all year round.

She would contact her mother when it was safe.

A smile lifted the corners of her mouth. Another elaborate plan. Ashley would put an item up for auction on eBay. Her mother knew what to look for, the buzzwords that they had agreed upon.

To ensure no one else attempted to lure either one of them into a trap, there would be a series of questions, each with a specific answer. Only Ashley knew the questions she would ask; only her mother knew her own. The questions weren't preplanned. But each understood that questions only the other could answer were necessary.

Once they had established contact, a reunion would be planned in whichever location appeared to be the safest.

So a move to California might end up more like a lengthy vacation than a relocation but that was okay with her. She couldn't wait to see her son again. Maybe, somehow, this time they could be together 24/7.

New identities. New home. The works.

A familiar sadness welled in Ashley. No matter how many identities they assumed or how many times they moved, there was always the risk that Desmond would just keep coming after them. The only hope she had of ever being safe was if he did die.

The idea of wishing another human being dead to save her son and herself felt wrong. Yet she couldn't help feeling that. If what Keith told her mother was true, Desmond was dying.

The only problem was, she doubted it would be anywhere near soon enough.

She sat up in her seat and ran her fingers through her hair. Almost ten o'clock. Fatigue had set in, draining her of strength as well as of her ability to fight over all those troubling thoughts.

Music could help. She started to reach for the radio, but hesitated. "Do you mind?"

He glanced at her, then shook his head.

Allowing her gaze to linger far too long on his profile, she shifted her attention to the radio. It took some time to locate a decent station. Soft rock was her favorite. She had no idea what he liked and she didn't ask, just tapped the scan button until a song she recognized drifted from the speakers.

She relaxed into her seat and let the music side-track her. Closing her eyes, she mouthed the words, let the rhythm lure her body into a little side-to-side motion that kept time with the beat.

As long as she was still alive, there was hope for hers and Jamie's futures. She wasn't about to let that die without a fight.

Another of her favorites filled the air and the music energized her, empowered her. She would get through this. No matter if the man sitting next to her was on her side or not. She would survive.

KEITH STOLE A LOOK at his passenger and felt his muscles tense when he'd been fairly certain his body couldn't get any harder.

Her eyes were closed. Those soft lips silently formed the words of the song, making him ache to taste them again. And that little rhythmic sway of her upper torso made him want to feel her moving against him like that.

He was pretty sure he would have taken her right on the clothes dryer back there if the mechanic hadn't interrupted.

Big, big mistake.

And he was barreling in that direction so fast he could hardly manage a deep breath.

He'd already taken an enormous chance by putting off giving up her location another twenty-four hours. His job had been so damned simple. All he had to do was find her. Attempt to persuade her to permit her son's father to see him. If that didn't work, he was to give her location to Brody and watch to make sure she didn't run until he arrived. So damned simple.

Here he was driving along this deserted road, more than likely making a major fool out of himself.

This so-called evidence might not exist.

His entire career could be over with this one assignment.

But he had to give her a chance.

Too many things didn't add up. Like the extreme measures she was willing to take to protect her son from Van Valkenberg. He'd mulled that over and over and came up with the same answer every time. There had to be some truth to her accusations.

If that were the case, how could he, in good conscience, turn over her location until the Colby Agency had looked into the matter more thoroughly. Which would infuriate the client. And, if Keith turned out to be wrong, make the agency look bad.

This was a mistake he didn't want to make, but he couldn't see any way around it.

His logical side had it all figured out. He would review the evidence, listen to her side of the story and then contact Victoria for her input. She wouldn't be happy that he'd taken this additional twenty-four hours on a hunch without discussing the full story with her, but what was done was done.

It might not be the route he'd intended to take, but it would work. Then he could at least say he'd given Ashley the full benefit of doubt.

That was the only way he'd be sleeping at night in the future.

He rubbed at his eyes and admitted that he could use some shut-eye about now. His head didn't hurt anymore. His hand went back to the wheel and he clutched it more tightly than necessary.

If he could just get his mind off her.

He allowed himself another peek. She was still quietly singing along with the music and doing that little dance with her torso. He wondered if she had any idea what effect she was having on him.

She seemed oblivious now but she sure as hell hadn't been a few hours ago. When she'd wrapped her arms around his neck and pulled him to her he'd almost lost his mind. Certainly the will to fight—to even think—had deserted him entirely.

He wasn't sure he'd ever met a woman who turned him on quite as much. Just taking a deep breath and smelling her subtle scent drove him mad with lust.

The silky feel of her hair and skin was the stuff fantasies were made of. Her body—well, there was something else to make a man lose all sense of protocol. Slender curves that beckoned him on every level.

He'd been nursing a major hard-on for about a hundred miles.

Her little foray into musical entertainment damn sure wasn't helping.

The car abruptly surged, then slowed.

His attention snapped to the dashboard. The service engine light flickered.

"What the hell?"

He pressed a little harder on the accelerator and the car lunged forward, the engine running smoothly now.

He relaxed a fraction. The gas gauge indicated plenty of fuel. The mechanic had filled the tank for him and he'd stopped about an hour ago and topped it off again.

The service engine light started to flash its warning once more and the car surged and slowed a second time. This time, no amount of acceleration did the trick. He had no choice but to guide the vehicle onto the side of the road. By the time he shoved it into Park, the engine had died.

"What's going on?" She turned off the radio.

"Don't know yet." He twisted the key in the ignition. The engine would turn over but it wouldn't crank. He swore.

The service engine light remained lit now.

Great.

He turned off the headlights, tucked the keys into his pocket and popped the hood before getting out. He surveyed the deserted road as best he could in the dark and moved to the front of the vehicle. As talented as he was in many things, he was no mechanic. He knew how to check the battery and various fluids. Even how to replenish those fluids.

But he knew absolutely nothing else about the workings of the monstrosity under the hood.

The light beneath the hood allowed a minimal visual inspection but unless the problem was glaringly obvious, it didn't really matter.

"What do you think is wrong?"

He glanced at the woman who'd gotten out of the car and was now standing next to him. The idea that she had done something else to the car rammed into his head with the same impact as that rifle butt the drug thug had wielded.

"What did you do?"

Her gaze collided with his, her eyes wide with innocence. "I didn't do anything. I swear."

"Dammit." He slammed the hood closed. "You promised you'd behave if I gave you twenty-four hours."

She probably couldn't see him fuming in the moonlight but just then he didn't care.

An incensed breath huffed across those sweet lips that he could see clearly with his mind's eye. What the hell was he doing letting her get to him like this?

"I had nothing to do with this." She flung an arm toward the car, the big movement apparent in the sparse moonlight. "Just because you don't know squat about how a vehicle operates isn't my fault. You figure it out."

She stormed back to the passenger side door and got in.

Okay, maybe she hadn't done this.

Or maybe that little show had been a ruse to throw him off.

He stamped back to the driver's door and dropped behind the wheel. The interior light stayed on long enough to allow the driver time to get the key into the ignition so he was able to shoot her a warning look. "If you're lying to me and I find out—"

"Just call somebody," she snapped, her lips a furious line, her eyes glittering with outrage.

The interior light faded into darkness.

Did he dare trust her?

Did it matter?

He reached into his pocket and pulled out his phone. Ben would send someone. No problem. All he'd have to do is give his location.

He hesitated as he was about to enter the number.

Was it routine to have to call for backup twice before an assignment was even complete?

Ben would surely let Victoria know he'd contacted him. Then Victoria would know what a mistake she had made pulling him out of research.

Keith had spent his entire life focusing on the details. In school he'd always been the teacher's pet. The smart kid that no one else related to. The geek, in a sense. Not as much of a nerd as Ben, but along that line.

He hadn't cared. He'd pretty much been a loner. Done his own thing. Some people called him shy, but actually he just preferred not to put himself out there. Trouble couldn't find him if he stayed out of its way.

Until a couple months ago, when Victoria had suggested he move into field work. He'd turned her down at first. But then, he'd started to think that maybe it was time he turned over a new leaf. Got involved. Put himself out there.

Why not?

Hell, he was thirty-two. Life was just going to pass him by if he didn't jump in and join it. His folks had been telling him that for years. Of course, this wasn't exactly what they'd had in mind, but they appeared to be happy for him.

Finding that tire wrench in his bag popped into his thoughts. He refused to screw this up. He could handle this without any help.

He closed the phone and tossed it onto the dash. He wasn't calling anyone until he was certain she didn't have anything to do with this. She wasn't going to make him look like an idiot again.

"It's late." He turned to Ashley, could barely make out her still ticked-off expression in the dark. "We should get some sleep. I'll call a tow truck in the morning."

Her mouth fell open. "You're kidding, right? We're going to sleep here? On the side of the road?"

"I do have a gun, in case you've forgotten. We'll be fine." The memory of those guys at the shack in the woods skipped through his head, but he evicted it. Just in case, he pressed the lock button. Of course, he didn't actually have any intention of sitting here all night.

For about ten seconds, he thought she might just come clean. Then she showed him that no matter how hard he tried, she was always, always one step ahead of him.

She hit the unlock button and wrenched her door open. "No way am I sitting here all night. I'll walk."

"Damn," he muttered, then got out and went after her.

"Don't even think about it," she warned when he moved up alongside her and was about to take her arm. She held onto the shoulder strap of her purse and just kept walking.

"You can't do this."

"Why can't I?" She didn't slow, didn't look back. "I've done it before."

A new blast of anger broadsided him. "If I find out you—"

She spun around to face him. He barely stopped before slamming into her.

"I told you I didn't do this." She stabbed him in the chest with her finger. "Stop trying to blame this on me!"

He manacled her hand, the contact only serving to ratchet up the tension already vibrating through him. "You've orchestrated every other disaster since I met you," he growled right back.

"Maybe you just can't handle the job without your pal in the trench coat rushing to your aid."

He shut her up with his mouth. He hadn't meant to let things go there, but, hell, he was only human. He couldn't take any more of her talk…but her lips, well they were a different story.

She shoved at his chest once, as if she didn't want him kissing her, but her resistance only lasted two or three seconds. She melted against him the way she had that first time they'd kissed, and every part of him responded.

The kiss went on until they were both gasping for breath. "We should—" he kissed her chin "—get back—" he kissed her cheek "—in the—" his lips traced her jawline "—car."

She hung her arms around his neck and dove in for more, determined not to let his lips get too far from hers. But he needed more. He lifted her and her legs went instinctively around his waist and, somehow, he found his way back to the car.

He opened a door, not caring which one, and crawled inside with her still clinging to him.

Somewhere in the back of his mind, *backseat* registered and he was glad. No steering wheel to contend with. He kicked his shoes off and tucked the toes of his left foot into the armrest and pulled the door shut as if he'd done it a thousand times. The accomplishment emboldened him all the more.

Her fingers fumbled with the buttons of his shirt. The scrape of her nails made him crazy with want. When her soft palms flattened against his chest, he groaned with pleasure.

Twice he told himself that this was a mistake... that he should stop this insanity...but he just couldn't do it. Couldn't do anything except exactly what he was doing.

Those wicked fingers found the waistband of his jeans and the button slipped loose...the metal-on-metal sound of his fly lowering made him shiver.

Grasping control of his runaway lust, he pulled her hands away, ushered them above her head with one hand while he had his turn. Slowly, he pushed her blouse up and over her bra. Her breasts heaved with the gasp of air she sucked in. He wished he could see more of her, but the sparse moonlight just wasn't co-operating. But his imagination was running damned wild. Those lace-covered mounds of creamy flesh made him want to taste the budding nipples he felt beneath his fingertips.

Her hips arched against his and she cried out with her own desire. "Hurry," she whimpered.

Torn between rushing for his sake and going more slowly for her pleasure as well as his own, he opted for the right thing.

He tasted her through the lace of her bra. She screamed. Her hands flew loose from his hold and tugged at his shirt in an attempt to draw his body closer to hers. He ignored her urgent prodding. He kissed his way down her torso, ravished the sensitive skin with his tongue. She squirmed and whimpered some more. The idea that he was making her feel exactly the way he did proved to be a heady sensation. He wanted to take his time, but each touch of his lips to her skin fueled his own urgency.

Ashley couldn't take any more of this. "Stop!" She pushed at his massive shoulders. His weight felt so good pressing against her, but it just wasn't enough.

"What's wrong?"

She glared into those amazing blue eyes glittering in the darkness as need, desire and flat-out frustration pushed her over the edge. "Look," she said breathlessly, "I haven't had sex in ten years. If you don't get down to business right now, I'm going to lose my mind."

He hesitated, but only for a second. Suddenly they were working to peel off her jeans. Why the hell had she worn the tightest ones she owned?

Gasping for air, hands fumbling for purchase, he managed to get them off. Her panties went next.

She shuddered with the intensity of the sensations as his hand glided over her thigh. "Hurry," she gasped.

He shoved his jeans down, not taking the time or the energy to shuck them entirely. He nuzzled between her thighs. And she almost came.

She screamed her impatience. He understood. But he didn't dive right in the way she wanted him to. He took it slow, one expanding inch at a time. Just when she was about to grab him by the hips and surge upward, he plunged fully inside her. Climax rippled through her. They both cried out this time.

How had she lived this long without this wondrous sensation in her life? This amazing feeling of completion?

His movements controlled to the point that he shook with the effort, he took her to climax again before he allowed himself the pleasure of joining her.

Nothing had ever felt this good.

Chapter Twelve

Keith leaned against the trunk and stared into the night. Man, he'd really made a mess of this.

He blew out a breath and crossed his arms over his chest to keep his hands from trembling. Major disaster.

How the hell had he fallen in love with Ashley Orrick in forty-eight hours?

Over and over during the past couple of days, he'd told himself that it was just lust. An attraction. Maybe even a little caveman protective instinct. Nothing else.

He hadn't allowed any of the minirelationships he'd entered into to move beyond superficial dating. Not since he'd come to work at the Colby Agency two years ago. He'd been too focused on his work.

If he took a long hard look at his love life to this point, he'd never really been deeply involved with any woman. It wasn't that he was old-fashioned, not at all. Sex was great. He liked it a lot. No, no. He loved it. But maybe he'd been saving his heart for just the right woman. Someone who made him feel... what he'd just felt in the backseat of this damned rented clunker of a sedan.

Not sexual gratification. There were a lot of ways to work off sexual frustration. He'd mastered most of them, including running until he exhausted himself. Nope, this feeling was something more. A high he'd never experienced before.

That left the age-old question of what now?

He was supposed to turn her location, if not her, over to the man whom she feared worse than death. His assignment included attempting to prod information about the whereabouts of her son out of her. He'd really fallen down on that job. Big-time.

Maybe he just wasn't cut out for field work. He'd worried that it was a mistake, but Victoria had assured him that he was ready. He had to confess, the idea had been flattering. He'd always been a sort of wallflower. Breaking away from a desk was a significant step for him. And look how he'd screwed up.

He scrubbed a hand over his face. The scent of the woman he'd just made love to lingered there, making his breath catch. He was being selfish. She surely had mixed emotions about what had just happened. Especially considering what she was going through.

The rear passenger door opened and she emerged from the car just then. Like him she folded her arms protectively over her chest and strode toward the trunk, looking pretty much anywhere but at him. He couldn't read her eyes, but the realization that she dreaded looking at him bothered him a good deal more than it should have.

She propped herself on the trunk next to him. "I suppose we should talk about this." She shrugged. "I…" She moistened her lips. "I know I'm okay. You know, clean. What about you?"

Startled at the question, he abruptly realized that he shouldn't be. "I'm…ah…clean, too. There's nothing you need to worry about." They hadn't used a condom. The idea of protection hadn't even crossed his mind. Just another place where he'd fallen down on his responsibilities.

She nodded. "Good. I'm not on the pill or anything, but…I was thinking—" she hitched her thumb toward the car "—in there that this time of the month was pretty safe. It should be okay."

He hadn't even thought of that. Incredibly, in spite of the risks they'd both just taken, tension started to vibrate through him all over again simply standing this close…hearing her tinkling voice.

"I want you to know," she said, turning to face him, "that I take full responsibility for what happened. I was…maybe a little needy."

"Ten years, huh?" he had to ask. That was a hell of a long time. Two years felt like forever. He couldn't imagine…the idea of how afraid she was of Van Valkenberg derailed that thought. No wonder she hadn't let herself get close to anyone else. It was a miracle she'd let him as close as she had.

She nodded. "I hope I didn't scare you or anything."

He choked back a laugh. "Believe me, there was nothing frightening about your eagerness." He wanted to reach out and pull her into his arms and just hold her. But would that only complicate the already complex situation? "And this is every bit as much my responsibility as yours."

"So, what do we do now?"

He blew out a breath. "I'll call Ben. He'll contact a tow service in the nearest town and we'll be rescued." Again, he didn't add.

Headlights came into view in the distance.

Keith squinted at the brightness as he tried to make out the type of vehicle headed in their direction.

"Hold up," Ashley said as she jogged to the side of the road.

Several seconds passed before he realized what she was attempting to do.

"Don't do that." He started toward her but she gestured for him to stay away. "Hitchhiking is dangerous," he argued.

She ignored him. Instead, she focused on waving

and jumping up and down to get the trucker's attention. Big rig running without a load. Damn, wasn't she worried that he wouldn't slow down, much less stop?

Apparently not.

Before he could grab her, she'd rushed into the middle of the road.

His heart lunged into his throat.

The squall of air brakes rent the air and, incredibly, the truck slid to a stop.

Ashley jumped onto the running board and spoke to the driver. Keith eased closer in an attempt to hear her words.

"The nearest service station would be great," she said.

He couldn't make out what the driver said.

"I really appreciate it." Ashley jumped off the running board and jogged over to where Keith stood, still a little shell-shocked. "Lock up the car. We've got a ride as far as we want to go."

He clicked the remote and followed her around to the passenger side of the big truck. When he'd assisted her up into the seat, he climbed aboard.

"You didn't tell me how cute he was."

Keith's gaze crashed into the driver's. Female. Fifty, maybe, with a lumberjack build.

"Yeah, he's cute." Ashley grinned at him. "But you have to keep an eye on him. He's a heartbreaker."

The older woman laughed loudly. "Aren't they all?"

With that insight, she shoved the truck into gear and roared forward.

As the speedometer's digital readout soared toward the triple digits, he reached for his seat belt.

He sat back and tried not to notice how fast they were going. Most of his attention was focused on the two women chatting as if they'd known each other forever.

During the next hour and a half, he learned several things he didn't know about Ashley Orrick. She adored strawberries and she never missed an episode of her favorite crime scene investigation program. The latter didn't surprise him in the least.

But it was the hurt in her voice when she talked about her son to the woman that damaged his defenses the most. She made up an elaborate story about how he was spending the summer with her folks at the beach. He loved the water, she explained. And the sand. Building sand castles was his favorite outdoor activity.

He relaxed, forgot all about the speed at which they were traveling. He was mesmerized by the sound of her voice and the stories she weaved, half-truths mixed in with covers to hide her true identity.

This was the life she had lived for ten years.

That had to have taken its toll.

It occurred to him that she fully anticipated never returning to the home she'd left in Waynesville.

Whatever life she'd built there was, as far as she was concerned, over. Now she sat, quietly telling about a new life, the one where she moved close to her folks in California.

His job was to see that California never happened, at least not until Van Valkenberg had departed this world. He wanted his son in Chicago, near him for his remaining days. Ashley was scared to death of him; she would never go for that. Not unless the law forced her to.

It was Keith's job to ensure she faced that legal battle if a cordial agreement couldn't be reached.

What did that make him?

The enemy.

The same kind of monster her mother had spoken of so vehemently.

And all this time he'd thought he was one of the good guys.

ASHLEY SCRUBBED the dingy mirror and stared at her reflection. They'd waited for three hours for the tow truck to get back with the rental. Now, the mechanic on duty was considering the problem.

It was almost 4 a.m. She hadn't slept at all.

Hadn't been able to.

She kept thinking about how it felt to make love with Keith. So far, she hadn't found the first word that even came close to describing it.

Amazing was far too generic to describe the experience.

Did he feel the same way?

That was a totally stupid question. She was his assignment, not his girlfriend.

Dark circles were painted beneath her eyes. She needed sleep, but she couldn't let her guard down. It wasn't that she didn't trust Keith to keep his end of this bargain, but she knew Desmond too well. He could send his own team in if things weren't happening on his timetable.

She shuddered at the thought of even seeing him again. He was sick. A total bastard.

"Don't think about him."

Kicking her troubles out of her mind for a while, she went about cleaning up a little. The rough paper towels made for less-than-luxurious washcloths, but just now she felt lucky to have them. She dug her brush out of her purse and tugged it through her hair.

She wanted to relish last night. Wanted to think about how incredible being with Keith had felt. But she had to get her head back on straight. They would be home soon. She'd show him the tape and see how he reacted.

Squeezing her eyes shut, she prayed he would be on her side. She desperately needed him to be.

She was so tired of being in this alone. That wasn't fair. She had her mother, Marla and Gina. But that wasn't the same as having a man who cared about you standing next to you.

Enough of that. She couldn't change the choices she'd made in her life. She'd go through all of it again, over and over, if it meant having Jamie.

He was everything to her.

She had to protect him. Keith didn't understand, she feared. And neither would a judge. He would only see that she had deprived a man of his son. Unless the evidence she had hidden was sufficient, she didn't have a chance proving what a monster Desmond was.

The thought of having to turn Jamie over to him for even a day terrified her.

Whatever it took, she couldn't let that happen.

A knock on the door made her jump.

She took a moment to calm herself. "Yeah?"

"The car's ready. You okay in there?"

She touched the door, wished she could touch the man. Lean on him the way she longed to. But she couldn't allow anymore lapses.

This was far too important.

SHE SAID NOTHING as they drove the final hour and fifteen minutes to her childhood home.

Keith had attempted to start a conversation a couple of times but she hadn't picked up the thread.

Dawn had arrived and he had to restrain the urge

to look at her far too often. He didn't want to make her feel any more uncomfortable than she already did.

He'd spent all those hours at the service station wrestling with what exactly the right thing to do was. Talk about a dilemma. He'd seriously put himself smack in the middle of one. Sadly, there didn't appear to be an easy out or fix for the situation.

As much as he'd like to venture into the subject with her, he sensed that she didn't want to go there.

The one conclusion he had reached despite his precarious position in all this was that he could not—would not—turn her or her location over to Van Valkenberg's people until he was certain it was safe to do so.

He turned onto the long gravel drive that led to the deteriorating farm house.

"Stop!"

The fierce emotion behind the one word had him engaging the brake even before the meaning registered.

"I want to walk from here."

He started to protest, but didn't see any reason to. She got out of the car and started walking toward the home where her parents had raised her until she went off to college.

Was this the first time she'd been home since she'd run away?

Ten years was a long time…for a lot of things.

Taking her time, she surveyed the land around the

home. It didn't take much imagination to deduce that things would look way, way different now. When she'd lived here, all the land for as far as one could see had belonged to her family. Now new homes dotted the landscape, marring the natural beauty.

Nor did it take a crystal ball to figure out the land had been sold off to help her and her son. That realization had to have a tremendous impact on her now that she could see the results for herself.

Instead of driving around her, he sat there and watched her move closer to the home that had once been a lovely place. It now stood in a state of disrepair that would make the most hard-core do-it-yourselfer wince.

Was guilt weighing heavy on her shoulders?

As she walked up onto the porch, he let the car roll forward until he reached the house. He parked and got out at the same time that she entered the front door.

He walked in while she was still standing in the living room, taking inventory of the changes.

The room was tidy, like the last time he'd been here. The furniture looked worn, but it was clean and well loved judging by the numerous throw pillows and afghans arranged to give it a fresher appearance.

She smoothed her hand over the back of her mother's chair. Keith remembered that Mary Orrick had chosen that seat when they'd talked a few nights ago.

At the fireplace, she lifted one of the framed photographs from the mantel and looked at it for a long time before moving on to the kitchen.

She opened the cupboard doors, one after the other as she moved through the room. When she reached the fridge, she opened the door and crouched down to peer inside.

Not much in the way of supplies.

Ashley pushed to her feet, closed the door and walked over to him. "How did she look?"

He chose his words carefully. The fragility in her eyes was killing him and he didn't want to say anything to do any additional damage. "She looked brave and very intelligent."

"Did she look well?" Her eyes searched his. She wanted to ensure he wasn't holding anything back.

He nodded. "Yeah, she looked well." A little thin, he didn't add. At the time, he didn't think anything of it. Most women preferred to be thin.

That seemed to appease her. "Good." She walked past him then and started up the stairs.

She stopped to view each framed picture on the wall, as if seeing an old friend for the first time in a long time.

At the top of the stairs, she opened and went through the first door. Keith followed.

She inhaled deeply. "It smells like her." A smile brightened her face. "I can't believe it's been so long since I've been here."

Every room in the house was inspected in this manner. He had to say he enjoyed the time in her bedroom. The old high school year books and cheer-leading trophies. That was something he hadn't known about her. She was Miss Popular in school. The total opposite of him.

When he asked why there weren't any pictures of her son, she explained that her mother kept those with her at all times. She never left anything related to the last ten years in the house. He could understand that.

After she'd had her fill of memory lane, she turned to him. "I guess we should get down to business."

"Whenever you're ready."

She hesitated at the door. "Keith, I want you to know that no matter what happens, I appreciate your patience. You've gone out of your way to be fair."

Enough. He couldn't do this without touching her. He pulled her close, tucked her against his chest. It felt right. "Whatever happens, I'll be there, right beside you."

She smiled, looked a bit teary-eyed. "Thanks."

Pulling free of his embrace, she took his hand and led him downstairs. In the kitchen, she got a butter knife out of a drawer, then sat down on the floor near the back door. She wedged the knife under a floor-board and pried the board up. She pulled up another and then another. He knelt next to her, noticed that the boards weren't nailed.

Beneath the boards was a lockbox. The kind people kept their wills and other important documents inside. Then she dug around in her purse and fished out the key.

The lockbox contained a single item. A videotape.

"This has your evidence on it?"

She nodded.

He stood, offered his hand to help her up. She took it, sending a protective feeling surging inside him.

The television set in the living room was equipped with a VCR. She turned both on and popped in the tape.

As the picture cleared, one of the images on the video was familiar. Desmond Van Valkenberg. He and a woman were engaged in seriously rough sex. Keith winced more than once at the brutality of the guy. He had to be disturbed to do this sort of thing.

Or maybe he just wanted to believe that because he wanted to believe Ashley.

As if reading his mind, she said, "There were hundreds of tapes like this."

The images on the screen faded to black. There was a second or two of nothing but gray lines, and then a new scene flickered into focus. Desmond and yet another young woman.

This time things got way out of hand.

Keith tensed. Ashley looked away.

Equal measures of indignation and outrage built as he watched the sick game play out.

When the intensity escalated farther out of control, Ashley muted the sound and turned to Keith. "She's the one who—"

"Is she dead?" He'd tried to pay attention to what Ashley was saying, but the images on the screen wouldn't let him turn away.

Her gaze shifted back to the screen. "I've asked myself that a thousand times."

Keith grabbed the remote and hit visual search so he could rewind to the exact spot where he'd thought for sure that Desmond had killed the woman. He hit Pause. "Look."

Ashley stared hard at the screen. "I know. She's not moving." She turned back to Keith. "This is what I'm talking about. I can't prove she's dead in that video, but she was reported missing two days later and then her body turned up two years later."

Keith crouched in front of the screen and peered more closely. "She looks dead to me. See—" he pointed to her face "—she isn't even blinking. Her eyes are open and she isn't blinking. The camera stayed on for another full minute and she didn't blink once. And I sure as hell didn't see her chest rise or fall."

"This is all I've got." Ashley crouched next to him. "Do you think it's enough?"

He turned to meet her gaze. "Absolutely." He stared back at the frozen screen. "No wonder he's been trying to find you. This could send him to prison."

The crunch of gravel followed by the sound of a car skidding to a stop outside jerked his gaze toward the window.

He and Ashley exchanged a look. "Did anyone know you were coming?"

She shook her head.

He pushed Stop on the VCR.

She was on her feet and at the window peeking out to see who'd arrived.

He reached beneath his shirt for his weapon and started toward the door.

Just before he reached it, she spun around, her eyes wide with shock or fear or maybe both. "You son of a bitch! You set me up!"

He pushed past her and looked out beyond the edge of the blind. Two goons had emerged from the car. He looked back at her. "Who are those guys?"

She looked at him with such disgust that it sliced right through his gut. "They're Desmond's men!" She shook her head as she backed away from him. "I can't believe you set me up."

Chapter Thirteen

"We don't have time to argue. Find some place to hide," Keith ordered. When she hesitated, he growled, "Now!"

Ashley hovered in the same spot for three more beats, trapped somewhere between devastated and mad enough to scream. How could he do this to her?

"Go!" he whispered.

Footsteps on the front porch propelled her into action. With one last glance over her shoulder, she left him standing there staring after her.

He had no right to look so worried.

This was his fault.

Not wasting any more time, she wiggled into the opening in the kitchen floor. There was barely enough room for her to fit between the floor joists, but she managed. The tricky part was getting the removed boards back into place properly and before those men got into the house.

She heard voices in the living room, Keith's and

another man's, just as she slid the final board into place. Her heart nearly stopped when she realized it wasn't down flush with the rest of the floor on one end. Holding her breath, she tapped it with her finger. Thankfully it slipped into place.

She let go of the air trapped in her lungs.

Thank God.

Then she remembered the video tape. Why the hell hadn't she grabbed the video tape? The voices grew louder and she held very still and listened intently to hear the conversation.

"I said she isn't here."

Keith. Why would he lie to the people who'd hired him?

"We know she's here, Mr. Devers. Let's not make this any more unpleasant than it needs to be. Mr. V. has given you ample opportunity and his patience has grown thin."

She vaguely recognized that voice. But both faces were familiar. She'd seen them before.

"If Mr. Van Valkenberg has a problem with my work, he needs to take it up with Mrs. Colby-Camp. That's the proper protocol, gentlemen."

Was it possible that he hadn't been in on this?

It sure sounded as if he were innocent.

"He's not going to cooperate, Marcus."

Marcus. She remembered that name. He'd been one of Desmond's right-hand men. A bodyguard of sorts.

Her heart rate picked up, making the blood roar in her ears. She held her breath in an attempt to slow it but it didn't work. If Keith wasn't the one who called and gave their destination away, this situation could become very dicey for him. Good thing he was armed.

But knowing he had a weapon didn't make her feel any better. He didn't seem like the type to shoot anyone.

"I think you're right."

She couldn't tell which of the men had spoken.

"Now just a minute."

Keith sounded tense or nervous.

"Don't move unless I tell you to, Mr. Devers, and this won't be nearly as unpleasant."

Ashley's heart stopped cold. They would kill him. She was suddenly very certain of that.

The heavy slap of footsteps coming into the kitchen made her freeze.

She prayed he wouldn't walk over the boards directly above her. If they were loose…

Whoever it was paused for a moment, then walked back into the living room. The conversation had stopped. What did that mean? Renewed fear seared through her veins. What if they'd hurt Keith already?

She listened, the pounding of her heart echoing in her head.

"Sit."

The man named Marcus had given the order.

"I'm certain Mr. Van Valkenberg would not approve of your tactics."

Oh, but you're wrong, Keith, she screamed silently. He just didn't understand what a monster Desmond was.

The front door slammed. Who went outside?

"You don't know Mr. V. very well, do you, Devers?"

"Apparently not. You're wasting your time here. Miss Orrick gave me the slip late last night. I was hoping she'd come back here looking for her mother."

Ashley stilled. He was going to get himself killed for her? Her chest tightened. She'd been running so long, doing everything possible to protect her son, that she'd forgotten what it was like to have to worry about anyone else. As much as she loved her mother, she'd had to let her fend for herself in order to ensure her son's safety.

All those new houses on their land…her childhood home's state of disrepair…the nearly empty cupboards. She had done this to her mother.

Tears burned at the back of her eyes.

The front door banged against its frame once more.

She cleared her mind of the past. It was the present that she needed to focus on.

"That'll do fine."

Marcus.

"Put your hands behind your back, Devers."

The unknown man.

God, they were restraining him. Her palms started to sweat. There was no telling what they would do before they killed him. Torture…

She had to do something.

Ashley tried to think. Her mother would take care of her son. She didn't have to worry about that. If she didn't get through this—and that had always been a possibility—she could hardly bear the idea that her son would be hurt, he would be safe with her mother.

The demands for her whereabouts grew louder. Keith continued to deny knowing where she was. Ashley thought she could hear someone going through the house. Upstairs, maybe.

She wished she had a cell phone so she could call for help.

It didn't matter now. Help wouldn't arrive in time.

Whatever happened next was up to her.

The first sounds of torture filtered through the cracks in the boards and her stomach clenched. The unmistakable smack of flesh against flesh, followed by an equally distinctive grunt.

The rhythmic *thwack-thwack* of someone coming down the stairs echoed next. Then, "She's not in the house."

More beating…more threats.

She couldn't listen anymore.

She had to act.

The first board was the hardest. It took every ounce of courage she possessed to shift it out of its slot. The ruckus in the living room escalated and she understood that she was out of time.

Careful not to make any unnecessary noise, she eased the rest of the boards out of her way and scrambled out of her hiding place.

She grabbed the broadest butcher knife from the block on the counter and walked straight into the living room.

"Stop!"

The scene seemed to freeze right in front of her.

Keith was the first one to recover. He shook his head at her decision to come out of hiding.

Her heart dropped into her stomach when she got a good look at his face. They'd beaten him good. Crimson had seeped into the bandage on his forehead, indicating they had purposely pummeled his old injury.

"Why hello there, Miss Ashley," Marcus said facetiously. As usual, the large man—he had to be six-three—wore a suit. Desmond always dressed up everything, even the whores he abused.

She'd always hated Desmond's minions, especially this one. The idea that those big, ugly hands had hurt Keith made her want to kill him. "The tape is over there." She pointed to the television. That was what they wanted. The evidence that could possibly put their boss away for life. That same evidence had served as her insurance all these years. She'd been certain he wouldn't want to risk the negative attention it would draw even if he could buy himself out of any trouble related to it. But she no longer needed it. Her son was out of reach. There was nothing else they could do to her. "Take it and leave us alone."

Marcus laughed. "You hear that, Buzz? She wants us to leave."

Buzz, the one whose name she hadn't remembered, shook his head. "Not going to happen." He was younger, maybe her age. He wore the same trademark I-work-for-the-richest-man-in-Chicago tailored suit.

Too bad there wasn't a warning label letting those who got too close know that these guys were armed and dangerous.

"I'm giving you the tape," she shouted, not doing a very good job of keeping her emotions in check. "What else do you want?"

Marcus smiled that fake smile of his. "We want the boy."

Terror jolted through her. "Why? He doesn't even know his father. Don't give me that ridiculous story about Desmond being ill and wanting to spend his last days with his son. I know that's a lie." She couldn't keep the contempt out of her tone.

"Ashley, don't."

Keith's plea was punctuated by a brutal punch to

his stomach. He bent forward as far as his restraints would allow.

"Shut up," Marcus said to him. "This doesn't concern you."

She wanted to run to Keith, but she didn't dare move.

"Mr. V. wants his boy. End of story. Now give us the location."

She tightened her fingers around the knife's handle. "I can't. I don't know where he is."

The surprise in Marcus's eyes sent victory soaring through her.

He moved around Keith and came toe-to-toe with her, ignoring the knife. "You *will* tell me."

She stabbed at him with the knife. He grabbed her wrist and wrenched it until she had no choice but to release her weapon. She bit her lip to prevent the cry that fluttered at the back of her throat.

He kicked the knife away. "Where's the boy?"

Her shoulders lifted and dropped. "I don't know."

"Tie her up and put her in the trunk," he said to his cohort. "We'll take her back to Chicago. Mr. V. will get what he wants out of her."

Buzz grabbed her by the arm and dragged her toward the door. She tried to jerk free but it was no use. The door closed behind them before she could look back at Keith one last time.

As the brute dragged her across the porch, she realized all she needed was her courage. This time would be no different than any other she'd planned for night after night for ten years. All she needed was her courage and the right plan.

KEITH WATCHED the door close behind Ashley. He had to get loose. If he didn't…

Marcus grabbed the video. "At least we didn't have to trash the place to find this." He laughed as if he'd just told the funniest joke of all time. "You see," he said to Keith as he headed back in his direction, "the funny part is, it didn't even matter. 'Cause we're gonna burn the place down with you in it."

Keith didn't bother mouthing off. He'd just get punched again. And he'd had about enough of that.

The other one, Buzz, came back inside carrying two gas cans. "We need anything else outta here?"

Marcus shook his head. "Take care of him." He jerked his head toward Keith. "I'm going outside to call Mr. V."

"Got it covered," Buzz assured him with glee in his tone as his partner took his leave.

Keith kept thinking that Ashley had been right all along. No one had known the truth, and he wasn't sure she could have convinced anyone with all that she knew about the bastard. It was too unbelievable.

"Who tipped you off?" That was one thing Keith had to know. How the hell did these scumbags find out where they were headed?

Buzz laughed as he splashed gasoline around the room. "Easy. We've been tracking you ever since you left her house the second time."

But no one knew they were going back to Ashley's house after the run-in with the drug makers.

"How did you know we were at her house?"

"Oldest trick in the book. We put a tracking device on your car when you went back to her house the second time. If you hadn't come back that second time, I don't think we would have been able to find you. Lucky for us, you showed up. Ironic, huh?"

Keith swallowed back the bitter taste of hate. "You had all your bases covered," he sneered.

"We always do. Mr. V. knew you had turned when he got the word that you'd asked for twenty-four more hours even after you located her."

He splashed gasoline onto Ashley's mother's chair.

Keith watched as he moved toward the far side of the room. Sweat rose on his skin. He had one chance here. He couldn't blow it.

When Buzz took his next step, putting him within range, Keith lunged to his feet as best he could tied to a dining room chair and charged the scumbag.

Keith hit him square in the side as the thug wheeled toward the sound of Keith hurtling at him.

They both went down.

Only one would be getting up.

Buzz had slammed headfirst into the hearth. A

couple of the framed photographs had fallen from the mantle and shattered on the brick that had absorbed the goon's impact.

Keith didn't have time to worry about whether Buzz was dead. As long as Buzz wasn't moving, that was all that mattered.

Keith rolled onto his knees and chest and attempted to get to his feet. The crash had broken the chair. He shook free of it and looked around the floor for the knife Ashley had been carrying. He had to angle the knife just right and it took a few seconds more than he would have liked. He cut the hell out of himself, but he sliced through the duct tape binding his hands.

He grabbed the gun they'd taken from him and eased to the window. Marcus was several yards from the house. Apparently he couldn't get reception any other way since he was still on his cell phone. Keith remembered that reception had been better nearer the road.

He slowly opened the door, treaded cautiously out onto the porch. The boards squeaked, and he had to be damned careful. When he got down the steps he moved faster, came right up behind the bastard still deeply absorbed in his phone call. He kept quiet until Marcus hung up.

"I'll need your phone and your weapon," Keith ordered. Part of him wanted to beat this guy the way he had been beaten, but there was no time.

Marcus started to slip his phone into his pocket and Keith moved in close behind him and nudged him with his gun. "Give it to me." When the man obeyed and then raised his hands in surrender, Keith tossed his phone as far as he could and said, "Now give me your weapon."

"You're making a mistake," Marcus warned.

Keith snatched the gun from him. "No. I made a mistake believing your boss. Now I'm doing the right thing."

Just to be sure, he patted Marcus down and ushered him toward the car. "Open it." He gestured to the trunk.

"I'll need the keys."

Keith pushed him toward the driver's side of the car, but reached in to get the keys himself, keeping a steady bead on the bad guy. He wasn't taking any chances.

He tossed him the keys and they moved back to the trunk. The instant the lid flew open, Marcus hurtled backward, landing hard on his back.

Keith stared first at the downed man, then into the trunk. He grinned, then yelped at the burn from his busted lip. Ashley had positioned herself so that when the trunk opened she could kick the hell out of whoever was standing there ready to grab her.

"Don't move," he ordered the guy on the ground.

Keeping one eye on Marcus, he helped her out of the trunk. Her hands and feet were bound with duct tape, so he had to lean her against the trunk. "I'll have to get a knife to cut you loose."

She nodded her understanding.

Before doing that, he gently pulled the tape off her mouth. She winced. So did he.

He grabbed the roll of tape. "I'll be right back." He said to Marcus, "Let's go."

Buzz had started to rouse when Keith hustled Marcus into the house. He quickly restrained Marcus, mouth first to shut him up and then his hands and feet. Then he took care of Buzz, giving him a matching ensemble of silver bracelets, wrists and ankles.

He grabbed his cell phone and the knife he'd used. Before walking out the door, he said to the two men, "Don't light any matches."

After cutting Ashley loose, he took her in his arms. Had to hold her. "Are you all right?"

She trembled in his arms. "I am now."

He held her that way for a moment, wanting her to feel safe. But they couldn't waste any time. He had to get in touch with Victoria and let her know what was really going on with Van Valkenberg.

He drew back from the embrace, didn't want to but knew he had to. "You look for the tape. It wasn't on Marcus so he must have stashed it in the car. I'm going to call this in—"

His cell phone chirped.

Ashley caught her breath.

"It's just a voice mail." He didn't remember hearing his phone but then he'd been a little busy the last hour or so. He reached into his jeans pocket and pulled it out. He checked the caller ID display. He'd missed a call from Ben.

He selected the option for listening to his mail. As soon as he'd reviewed the message he would call in this latest development.

"Keith, I guess you're busy but you need this information like, two hours ago. We have a situation here. A woman claiming to be Miss Orrick's mother just called and she insists that she must speak to her daughter. She was pretty hysterical. But from what I could tell, the boy ran away and she thinks he might be headed to Marla Beck's house in Springfield. You think there's anything to this? Let me know what steps you intend to take. Brody's not taking any of this too well. He wants the boy found like right now. He just called and demanded an update. He is furious at the idea of the kid being out there on his own. Victoria kind of left me…"

Keith closed the phone. Didn't need to hear the rest of the message. Dread kicked him in the chest. He had no idea who Marla Beck was but if there was any truth to the call at all, Van Valkenberg's people already knew where the kid might be headed.

Ben was right. He'd needed this information two hours ago.

Chapter Fourteen

"We'll never get there in time." Ashley chewed on her thumbnail, too sick with worry to sit still.

"We'll get there," Keith promised as he wheeled into South Bend Regional Airport.

There had been no time for anything else. Keith had called Ben and ordered the Colby Agency's jet. They had to get to Springfield before Desmond's thugs.

Ashley squeezed her eyes shut and prayed again that God would protect Jamie.

What was he thinking, taking off like that?

He knew better.

Her mother had called the Colby Agency back and said it looked as if he'd taken a bus. He'd left in the middle of the night. She hadn't even realized he was gone until she'd gone in to waken him for breakfast.

He'd learned his lessons well from his mother.

Disappear when it was least expected. And be prepared.

She could have prevented this. She should never have allowed that devil Desmond to rule their lives. There had to be something she could have done differently.

"Here we go." Keith parked the car in the area designated for corporate flights. He turned to her. "Don't beat yourself up, Ashley."

Those blue eyes looked almost as worried as she felt. Could he possibly care about what happened to her son? It had been so long since anyone besides the three people close to her had offered anything, much less cared.

"You did what you thought was best. I would have done the same."

She nodded, couldn't muster the necessary skills for speech.

"Let's get on that plane and go find your son."

His smile brought tears to her eyes. He did care. No way was this fake.

She nodded, grabbed her purse and reached for the door handle. He was at her door before she'd realized he'd gotten out of the car. Boy, she really was out of it. Shock, she decided. Or plain old fear.

If anything happened to her son…

No. She got out of the car. She refused to consider that possibility. She would find him first.

They boarded the plane and the pilot informed

them that takeoff would be in twenty minutes. The flight would take less than an hour.

She prayed. Told herself that she had trained Jamie well when it came to dealing with strangers. He would be fine. She had to believe that.

Keith offered her a bottle of water and she accepted it. Her throat was so dry, swallowing proved nearly impossible.

"There's a wide variety of snacks, if you're hungry," he offered.

She shook her head. "No thank you. I couldn't."

He nodded his understanding and opened his own bottle of water. She knew he was hungry, but he didn't get anything for himself.

"You should eat, if you're hungry." He shouldn't hold out just because she wasn't having anything.

"I'm good."

Where had guys like him been ten years ago?

She had to turn off her brain for a few minutes. Too much to worry about.

She desperately wanted her son to grow up happy. To meet a wonderful girl and fall in love the way it was meant to be. Happiness, a priceless commodity.

And sometimes so far out of reach.

The plane started to roll forward. Anticipation made her heart start to fly even before the plane got off the ground.

A telephone rang. Not a cell phone.

Keith reached toward the table next to his chair and lifted a receiver out of a built-in niche.

Taking a private jet was far ritzier than going coach on a commercial jetliner.

Lush carpeting. The seats, all six of them, were like elegant leather recliners that swiveled.

And more she hadn't seen.

She'd bet the restroom was far nicer, as well.

"I understand. Thank you."

Keith hung up the receiver and his gaze settled on hers. Ashley's heart dropped all the way to the thick carpet around her feet. There was news. *Please, please, God, let it be good.* She couldn't read what he was feeling. Was the news good…or bad?

"That was Ben. The driver of the bus into Springfield just confirmed that your son arrived safely and exited the bus at the downtown station approximately one hour ago."

"Thank God." The words were scarcely a burst of air. At least he was safe up until that point.

"There's something else."

There was something in his expression this time that made every part of her being go utterly still.

"When I called Ben and updated him on what went down at your mother's, I asked him to look into Van Valkenberg's state of health. At this point, we have to assume he may have lied about everything.

But, he didn't lie about one part. He is dying. That has been confirmed."

Part of her felt glad to hear that. Her lips trembled and she fought back her tears. The bastard deserved to die.

"But all hope isn't lost. The problem is his heart. All he needs is a suitable donor."

Terror wrapped around her; she couldn't breathe. The full impact of Keith's statement hit her.

"That's why he wants my son. He wants his heart."

THE HOME owned by Marla Beck gave every appearance of being deserted. Backup—A.J. Braddock and Simon Ruhl, two of the Colby Agency's best—had met Keith at the airport. The local authorities had been alerted and were on standby in the event official assistance was needed. The videotape was being hand-delivered to the Chicago District Attorney's office at that very moment. Whatever involvement Van Valkenberg had in a decades-old murder was out of the Colby Agency's hands.

But the man himself, that was another story.

Keith intended to personally see that he didn't get anywhere near Ashley or her son.

"You should touch base with Marla now that we're here." Her minivan was not in the driveway. Since Ashley no longer had her cell phone, there had been no way for Marla to contact her. If they were lucky, Jamie would be with her by now.

Her hands shaking, Ashley accepted the cell phone he offered and entered Marla's cell number. "Marla." Her breath caught and her eyes closed a moment as she struggled to hold on to her composure. "Is Jamie with you?"

The absolute terror in Ashley's voice tore Keith apart. His fingers clenched into fists of rage at the idea of what Van Valkenberg had planned for the boy. Of what he had put both of them through for the past decade. Selfish bastard.

Ashley pressed her free hand to her mouth for a moment and Keith knew the news wasn't good.

When she'd regained control of her emotions, she pleaded with her friend, "Keep looking, okay? I'll call you if we have any news on this end."

She pressed the End Call button and handed the phone back to Keith. "She's looked everywhere. All the places we told him to go in the event of something like this." She shook her head, tears shining in her eyes. "Nothing."

Keith wanted to hold her. To promise her everything would work out in the end…but he couldn't lie to her. She'd lived with enough lies already.

"We should check this house just in case," A.J. suggested.

A.J. was right. "Definitely." He turned to Ashley.

"You stay here with Simon. A.J. and I will make sure the house is clear. Just in case."

She nodded, her eyes glazed with worry.

His fury barely contained, Keith, with A.J.'s assistance, searched the house. Three-bedroom, two-bath ranch style. It didn't take long. And they found nothing. He even asked Ashley to come inside to check any place they might have overlooked. Allowing her to go into the boy's room turned out to be a mistake. She couldn't contain the tears any longer.

As he ushered her out the front door, his cell phone rang again. He flipped it open. "Devers."

"We have movement at the mansion."

Ben. He and another Colby Agency investigator, Todd Thompson, were watching the Van Valkenberg estate.

"A limo has just pulled out. We're going to follow it and see what Van Valkenberg is up to."

"Thanks, Ben. Keep me posted."

Keith put his phone away and filled Braddock in on what he'd learned. Ashley listened, but didn't make any comments. She'd almost gone as far as she could go. They had to find her son. Soon.

"We're missing something," he said more to himself than to Ashley or A.J. "I don't see how it's possible, but it feels like he already has the boy."

Ashley's fear visibly escalated. "Is that possible?"

Braddock rubbed his chin thoughtfully. "I guess

it's not impossible." To Keith, he said, "Do we know where Van Valkenberg's private jet is? That could give us somewhere to go from here."

"The last time I checked, it was still in Chicago, but I'll confirm there hasn't been any change." Keith put in the necessary call. Less than five minutes later, they had the information.

Van Valkenberg's private jet had landed at a private airfield just outside Springfield more than an hour ago. Their man in Chicago was left out of the notification loop.

"Someone should stay here in case the boy shows up," Keith said quickly, a plan forming rapidly in his mind. "The rest of us should head to the airfield."

Simon nodded his agreement with that strategy. "I'll stay here."

Ashley stared at the men as they talked. Keith had a bad feeling that shock had begun to delay her reactions. But there was no time to waste ensuring that she understood what they were about to do. The airfield was twenty minutes away. Anything could happen in twenty minutes.

ASHLEY SAT VERY STILL in the backseat. She didn't dare move or talk or even think. If she allowed her mind to go in any direction, it would only nurture the devastation roiling in her belly, threatening her flimsy hold on composure.

Please, God, she prayed, *don't let them hurt my baby.*

Keith and his associate, the man named Braddock occupied the front seat of the car. Neither spoke. Ashley was glad. She didn't want to talk. Talking required thinking. She just couldn't do that right now. She only wanted her son back.

As Braddock made the turn onto the road that led to the airfield, Keith's cell phone sounded again.

"Devers."

Ashley watched him, wrung her hands as anxiety tightened its hold on her throat. She prayed it was good news.

"I don't care what you have to do, Ben, get in there." Pause. "I don't know. Fake a heart attack, but do something."

Keith closed his phone then. He shifted in the seat so that he could look at her. "Van Valkenberg has just arrived at a private surgical clinic."

A new wave of fear washed over Ashley. "They're getting ready." Horror twisted in her chest. "They must have Jamie…otherwise preparations wouldn't be necessary."

Keith tried to comfort her with his eyes, but there was no way he could. Nothing could make her feel better now. Nothing but her son safely back in her arms.

The cell phone's ring shattered the tension again. "Devers."

Ashley held her breath.

"I understand. We're almost there." He closed the phone. "Van Valkenberg's jet is scheduled to take off in fifteen minutes."

Braddock didn't stop at the entrance gate. A guard burst out of the guard shack but Braddock didn't slow.

Ashley sat on the edge of her seat, her heart knocking against her rib cage. They had to get to Jamie before that plane took off.

"There!" Keith pointed to a hangar up ahead. "That's the hangar number."

Braddock roared up to the hangar and slammed the vehicle into Park. All three poured out of the car. Ashley felt as if her movements were stiff, surreal, happening of their own volition. Her thoughts were frozen, that same prayer echoing over and over inside her head.

Keith ushered her back toward the car. "Stay back, Ashley. We can handle this better with you safely out of the way."

"I'm going with you." Nothing he said could change her mind. Nothing.

"Let's go," Braddock urged. "There's no time to argue."

The sound of car engines roaring in the distance, security most likely, lent more urgency to his words.

"Stay behind me," Keith ordered.

Ashley managed a nod.

They raced to the hangar. The plane sat on the

tarmac beyond the looming building. Portable stairs had been rolled up to meet the open door.

Ashley recognized the man climbing the stairs. Brody.

He rushed up the stairs after catching sight of them.

Keith hit the bottom of the stairs first, didn't pause, just bounded up. Braddock was right on his heels. Ashley hurried up the steps next, her heart thumping painfully.

She prayed again that she would find her son safe.

Keith charged the closing door, barely managed to push through. Braddock disappeared inside right behind him.

Ashley, her breath sawing in and out of her lungs, didn't hesitate. She barreled through the door right behind them.

The first thing her eyes encountered was the three men engaged in a kind of standoff with Keith and Braddock, weapons drawn.

"You're trespassing, gentlemen," one of the men said. "Now kindly leave this aircraft. The pilot is already locked in the cockpit and prepared to take off."

A frantic scream rent the air.

"Jamie!" Ashley instantly zeroed in on the direction from which the sound came.

She bolted past Keith and Braddock; not even Desmond's three thugs moved quickly enough to stop her. She burst through the door and found herself in a private compartment much smaller than the cabin where the others were. Brody had positioned Jamie in front of him like a shield. His weapon was trained on Ashley.

"Take another step and I'll shoot you right in front of your son."

Fury obliterated any fear she had felt before. "How could you do this? I knew you were a lowlife bastard, but I didn't think you would stoop to murdering a child." Just then she saw the man wearing a white lab coat cowering in the corner...then the bed...and finally the medical equipment. Her breath whooshed out of her lungs. They had intended to prepare her son en route.

"You don't know what you're talking about," Brody argued. "Your son is ill. Just like his father. We're trying to help him. That's what this has all been about."

He looked frazzled, unaccustomed to doing the dirty work himself.

"I don't believe anything you say," she snarled, a lioness determined to protect her cub. "Let my son go and maybe you can get immunity by telling the truth about your boss."

Brody shook his head. "I'll die first." He looked at Ashley for a moment. "And I'll take you with me."

Oddly, she wasn't afraid. She smiled at her son, gave him a wink and did the last thing Brody would have expected—she dropped to the floor.

Her son bit Brody's arm. His hold loosened and her son dropped to the floor as well. The gun's blast thundered in the small compartment.

Before Brody could fire another shot, Keith had his weapon leveled on the man, "Drop it!" he ordered.

For two seconds that stretched out like eternity, Ashley feared Brody wouldn't cooperate, but then he did. The moment his weapon was in Keith's hand, Jamie ran over to her. They hugged and hugged. She kissed him over and over until he cried, "Mom! Enough with the kisses," and wiped his face.

Thank God she had her child back safe and sound.

She owed one man for making it happen, for believing in her.

He smiled down at her, didn't try to intrude on the mother-and-son reunion. There would be time to work things out with Keith later.

ASHLEY SAT on the swing of the front porch where she'd grown up.

The smell of her mother's cookies baking wafted through the open windows.

God, it was good to be home.

Jamie chased a chicken around the yard. She had to get that boy a dog. Now that they were on the farm, she could do that. She couldn't have him chasing her mother's chickens around; otherwise they'd never lay any more eggs.

School would start in a couple of weeks and Jamie would meet new friends. Maybe he'd even have some of the same teachers she'd had.

Life was good.

At long last.

Brody had lied about her son having an illness. A team of specialists had evaluated Jamie and he was as fit as a fiddle. Brody had come up with that excuse for his actions, claiming he had no idea what Desmond was really up to. But the D.A. wasn't buying his cover story, the last she'd heard.

A car speeding down the long drive left a cloud of smoke in its wake. Ashley smiled. Now life really was perfect. Keith was here.

He'd promised to drop by and check on them. She hadn't seen him since that day at the airfield outside Springfield. They'd talked on the phone a couple of times but she'd been so busy helping her mother get the house back into shape and getting Jamie settled, there just hadn't been time to talk at length.

It felt like eons since she'd seen him.

They'd both had so much to do and they'd decided that a little time apart would be best.

Stressful situations often brought people together who weren't really in love with each other; the reaching out was more about survival. She and Keith had needed some time and distance to make sure what they'd shared was real, not just a desperate act of survival.

He got out of the car and waved at Jamie. Jamie smiled and waved back. Ashley liked that her son appeared intrigued by Keith.

"Supper'll be ready in ten minutes!" her mother called from inside the house.

Ashley grunted a response. She couldn't take her eyes off the handsome man striding toward the porch long enough to give a decent answer.

"The house looks great," he said as he climbed the steps.

"Thank you." It certainly did. She and her mother had seen to the revamping of the whole house in the past two weeks. They'd hired a dozen renovation experts to get out here and get the job done. There were still a few things on the list, but the major problems were history now. All thanks to a very generous settlement from Desmond. He was awaiting trial, though most who knew him speculated that his heart would never hold out for the duration of the proceedings. Ashley could only assume that he hoped his generosity would sway the jurors when they were deciding his fate.

"Everything looks great," Keith said as he strode across the porch toward her.

She blushed as she stood to greet him. "So do you." No more bandages or bruises. He looked amazing.

"Can we talk a few minutes before dinner? I heard your mom sounding the warning."

Ashley smiled. Her mother would forever more be overprotective of her. "Sure." She took his hand and tugged him down onto the swing with her. Instinctively, she checked on her son who was galloping around the yard. He was so happy.

"I was thinking," Keith began.

Ashley shifted to face him. "Let me go first."

He nodded, his smile almost taking her breath.

She reached into her jeans pocket and pulled out a simple gold band and turned back to him. "I'm not sure of the proper etiquette here, but I'm not getting on my knees for this." She had to smile at his astonished look. "Will you marry me? You'll get a son and a live-in mother-in-law to boot. But I promise you'll never be bored."

That smile widened, took her breath all over again. "I guess I should have seen this coming. You always have a plan in place. Always one step ahead of me."

"Damn right." She took his hand, poised the ring above the proper finger. "So what's it gonna be, Mr. P.I.? Are you going to help me salvage my honor?"

"How can I say no?"

She slid the ring onto his finger. It wasn't exactly an engagement ring—she'd skipped right to the wedding band—but it would work.

"My turn," he said, not to be outdone.

He withdrew a small velvet box from his shirt pocket. Unlike her, he did drop down onto one knee.

Her heart took a running leap and practically jumped out of her chest. "Ashley, will you be my wife? Allowing me to be your son's father? And your mother's favorite son-in-law?"

She giggled at the last. "Only if you kiss me right now."

Only too happy to oblige, he kissed her long and deep, allowing her to feel all the love in his heart.

"Are we going to eat or what?" her mother called through the screen door.

They laughed, their lips still touching.

This, Ashley realized as she looked into Keith's eyes, was how fairy tales were supposed to end.

With the girl getting the guy.

Chapter Fifteen

Victoria closed the file on the Van Valkenberg case.
The final reports were done. Desmond Van Valkenberg would never spend a day in prison. His money
had bought him house arrest, considering he had only
a few days to live. The upside, however, was that he
would be closely watched by prison guards whose
salaries the state required him to pay.

Victoria shook her head sadly. His father would
be so disappointed in him.

It was late. She should call it a day. Everyone else
had gone home except Mildred. Victoria had to smile.
Faithful Mildred would never go home as long as
Victoria was still in the office.

Victoria rose, switched off the lamp on her desk
and pushed in her chair. Her purse and briefcase in
hand, she headed for the door.

She sincerely hated losing Keith, but his heart was
now in Indiana with the woman he loved and her son.

He and Ashley had many plans, none of which included his coming back to work at the Colby Agency.

Oh well. Victoria wouldn't dream of standing in the way of true love.

Mildred was just shutting down her computer as Victoria strolled out of her office.

"Ready to call it a night?" she asked.

Mildred nodded. "I think it's time."

"Big plans this weekend?" Victoria asked as the two made the journey down the long corridor to reception and the elevators there.

"Oh, nothing special."

But Victoria knew from the twinkle in her eyes that there was definitely something special on the agenda.

"You say hello to Dr. Ballard for me," Victoria offered as she pressed the call button for the elevators.

"I will. Lucas is returning tonight?" Mildred asked, shifting the spotlight from herself.

Victoria felt a surge of tingly sensations start deep in her belly at the mention of her husband's name. He'd been away a couple of days and she looked forward to his return with immense anticipation. Lucas always made his first night back home after being away very special. She shivered inside. Very, very special.

"He should be waiting for me when I get home."

The elevator doors glided open and the two stepped into the waiting car.

"I imagine we'll both have exciting weekends," Mildred suggested.

Victoria watched the doors close, blocking out the view of the agency she loved. She shifted her attention to her longtime friend and assistant. "Very exciting," she said with a knowing smile.

Mildred returned that knowing smile with a perceptive one of her own.

They rode in silence the rest of the way to the lobby, both anticipating the men in their lives and a breath-stealing weekend full of romance.

Both knew one thing for an absolute certainty: a woman was never too old for a little romance.

* * * *

Look for A Colby Christmas *this December for a very special holiday story from Debra Webb and Mills & Boon!*

Don't miss Past Sins *by Debra Webb*
available in August 2007.
Here's an exclusive sneak preview…

Past Sins
by Debra Webb

Once the convertible top was locked into place, she slid out of the seat and headed inside. The pleasant smell of her favorite white-wine sauce filled her nostrils the moment she stepped through the front door. Linguini and chicken, a staple of Jeffrey's culinary repertoire, would be on the menu. In addition to the pleasant aroma, classical music greeted her, the elegant notes playing softly in the background and making her feel immediately more relaxed.

"I'm home!" She almost laughed at the cheesy way she sounded. If she'd only tacked on the "honey" she would have been a living, breathing cliché. Olivia Mills had never been accused of being a stock quotient. Had that changed in the past three years along with everything else about her life? Evidently so. But there were definitely worse things. A lot worse.

"In here!" accompanied a rise in the tempo of the brass, strings and ivory keys.

Her stomach rumbling, she followed the smell into the kitchen. Hesitating at the door, she watched Jeffrey, engrossed in the preparation of a rich green salad. He paused in his work to dump the linguini into boiling water then turned back to slice fresh tomatoes into thin slivers just the way she liked them. He had very nice hands. Long, artist fingers. But the thing she liked best about him was his infinite patience and unconditional trust.

Two things she'd never been able to master herself. Her patience had never been that noteworthy, unless she was billing by the hour. And trust, well, she'd never trusted anyone. Still didn't…but she tried. Jeffrey made her want to try.

"Rough day?" he asked without looking up.

"Not so bad."

He would ask her about lunch next.

"Did you have lunch with Liz?"

"She had to cancel." Liz was a colleague with whom she lunched once or twice each month. They were about the same age, both single. The other woman was pleasant but, to be brutally honest, they had nothing in common other than profession. Still, socializing within the profession was expected. Fitting in dictated certain behaviors on her part.

With her and Jeffrey it was basically the same conversation every night. How was your day? Anything interesting happen at lunch? The only variable was whether she got home first to start dinner. Comfortable. Easy.

A trickle of trepidation seeped into her veins, making her pulse rate increase and reminding her that complacency was a weakness. Weakness was dangerous. All afternoon she'd been experiencing these sensations that alternated between urgency and hesitancy. Strange.

"Too bad. I understand she had some gossip to pass along," Jeffrey said, tugging her full attention back to him. He glanced at her and smiled that familiar, charming smile that had drawn her to him in the first place. "Wine?"

She nodded and he stopped his salad preparations long enough to pour her a stemmed glass of chardonnay.

Annoyed that she couldn't stay focused tonight, she moved to the island and accepted the drink. "Gossip?" she asked, feigning interest. Her heart rate's refusal to drop back to a normal level frustrated her further.

Jeffrey placed the glass in her hand. "She's leaving her position at Whitworth Clinic."

Olivia made the expected sound of disbelief. "What brought that on?" She listened as Jeffrey launched into the explanation that Liz's significant other had no doubt passed along to him. In Olivia's experience, men did a lot more talking about secrets than women did. She found this apparently common phenomenon among the civilian population amusing—or maybe it was just that her life before had been so vastly different. Whatever the case, there were times when she actually managed to feel intrigued by the juicy gossip floating about their social circle.

For some reason, today just wasn't one of those days. Today she had to pretend. It had been so long since she'd had to do that….

"What about you?" she asked when he'd completed his dissertation on the subject of their mutual friend's abrupt decision to move to a rival clinic. "Anything interesting happen in the world of research today?"

Dr. Jeffrey Scott was employed by one of the country's foremost pharmaceutical research corporations. Though the corporation was strictly private—no government affiliations whatsoever—what he did deep within the bowels of that facility was top secret. That was the part of their relationship that she related to the most readily.

He shrugged. "Nothing notable."

She hummed a note of acknowledgment and sipped her wine. "I think I'll change."

He reached for the next vegetable in need of slicing. "Ten minutes. Don't be late."

She produced a smile and turned away from the domestic scene.

This was her life. Comfortable. Easy. But there were times, like now, when she felt out of place. As if she didn't really belong here in this house… with this man. She downed a gulp of wine in hopes of bolstering the facade of happiness she'd worked so hard to veneer into place over the past three years.

"Don't think about it," she scolded softly as she tossed her purse onto the table in the hall. Allowing a patient's session to prompt this much anxiety was not her usual response. She was stronger than this.

The journey through her home was taken slowly. She surveyed every detail as if for the first time. Anything to get her mind off these ridiculous feelings of apprehension.

She had updated the house immediately after moving in. Gutted the place, actually. Sparing no expense, she had wanted a relaxing yet sophisticated living space. The interior decorator she'd hired had taken great pains with the decor and the furnishings had accomplished that goal. Using *things* and everyday decisions to fill the emptiness in her life had worked as an excellent distraction at first. Eventually it was not enough. She'd turned her attention elsewhere.

Dating had proven a practical trial for occupying her time for a while. However, no one had lasted beyond date number three until Jeffrey. She tossed her double-breasted suit jacket onto the king-size bed in their room and strode into the walk-in closet to find something more comfortable.

It wasn't that she'd fallen in love with Jeffrey. He'd simply fit nicely into the life she'd created for herself. He was reliable, kind and always considerate. He made no complicated demands. Simple was her new motto, after all.

Pink silk lounge pants and a matching camisole replaced her skirt and button-up blouse. The tile of the en suite bath felt cool beneath her bare feet, a welcome respite after wearing stilettos all day.

Once she had taken the pins from her French twist, she brushed through her long dark hair until it glistened around her shoulders. If she really took the time to consider her reflection, she would have to admit that she looked the same as before. Her hair was longer and darker, but otherwise she'd changed very little. Same green eyes. No additional wrinkles to speak of for a woman closer to forty than thirty. It was everything else in her life that had altered.

She hissed a breath of impatience. Why couldn't she stop this? She hadn't had this much trouble focusing since…since the beginning.

She grabbed her empty glass and headed back to join Jeffrey.

He'd set the dining table. Flowers, candles and the lovely white bone china they used every day. He placed the salad bowl in the middle of the table next to the linguini and white-wine sauce before he looked up.

"You need another drink."

He moved to her side to remedy that situation without her having to say a word. That was another thing she enjoyed about Jeffrey. Making her happy appeared to be his single goal when they were together. She should be grateful.

She was.

"Smells heavenly." She thanked Jeffrey for the refill and settled into the chair he pulled out.

He took his own seat directly across from her and lifted his glass. "To us." He smiled as their glasses clinked. "And a lovely evening."

She returned the smile and drank deeply from her wine.

Now was all that mattered.

Her new life…this moment.

The unmistakable sound of her cell phone chimed from the hall. She groaned.

"Don't answer it," Jeffrey suggested, looking mildly annoyed at the intrusion.

Olivia sat her glass down. "I shouldn't." She took a deep breath and rose from her chair. "But one of my patients is having a crisis. If he needs me…"

Jeffrey rolled his eyes but said nothing as she left the table without finishing the statement. He understood her dedication to her work even if he didn't like it at times. He was every bit as dedicated as she was.

She walked to the hall table and fished her phone from her bag. Jeffrey was right. She shouldn't answer. If it was one of her patients, he could leave a message.

The display flashed an icon she didn't remember seeing before. She frowned as she attempted to remember what it meant.

Then she knew.

Never count on anything to last.

FREE!

4 Books
and a surprise gift!

We would like to take this opportunity to thank you for reading this Mills & Boon® book by offering you the chance to take FOUR more specially selected titles from the Intrigue series absolutely FREE! We're also making this offer to introduce you to the benefits of the Mills & Boon® Reader Service™—

- ★ **FREE home delivery**
- ★ **FREE gifts and competitions**
- ★ **FREE monthly Newsletter**
- ★ **Exclusive Reader Service offers**
- ★ **Books available before they're in the shops**

Accepting these FREE books and gift places you under no obligation to buy, you may cancel at any time, even after receiving your free shipment. Simply complete your details below and return the entire page to the address below. You don't even need a stamp!

YES! Please send me 4 free Intrigue books and a surprise gift. I understand that unless you hear from me, I will receive 6 superb new titles every month for just £3.10 each, postage and packing free. I am under no obligation to purchase any books and may cancel my subscription at any time. The free books and gift will be mine to keep in any case.

17ZEF

Ms/Mrs/Miss/Mr ....Initials ....

Surname ....

Address .... **BLOCK CAPITALS PLEASE**

....

....Postcode ....

Send this whole page to:
UK: FREEPOST CN81, Croydon, CR9 3WZ